Red Card

Paul Cockburn

Virgin

The stories so far. Other books in the Team Mates series (in order):

Overlap
The Keeper
Foul!
Giant Killers
Sweeper
Offside
Penalty

First published in Great Britain in 1997 by
Virgin Books
an imprint of Virgin Publishing Ltd
332 Ladbroke Grove
London W10 5AH

A catalogue record for this book is available from the British Library.

ISBN 0 7535 0084 1

Typeset by Galleon Typesetting, Ipswich
Printed and bound by
Mackays of Chatham PLC

One

The noise from the other table grew louder. Chris tried to stop looking, but he couldn't help himself.

Three men were sitting about two or three metres away. One of them had his back to Chris, but since he didn't have as much to say as his mates, that didn't make much difference. All Chris could really tell was that he was tall, dark haired, and giggled like a girl.

The other two guys were much less pleasant. The one tucked into the corner was a small bloke with greasy blond hair hanging limply from his skull. He had very pale skin and a thin slash of a mouth. This twisted into one of two shapes depending on whether he was speaking (twisted upper lip, bright teeth) or grinning at his mate's comments (slightly curved, with the lower lip hidden behind his teeth). He liked to bang his hand on the table when he told a joke.

The third of the trio was short too, and made himself look even smaller by the way he sprawled in his chair, feet up on another seat, head drawn down into his shoulders like a turtle. He had brown hair, razor cut along the sides and back, and a small tattoo of a fish on his neck. His eyes flickered round the room nervously. Occasionally they would fix on someone, daring them to interfere.

Three complete losers. Their anger and spitefulness spilled all over the restaurant, fuelled by beer and the fact that they were a long way from home. There seemed to be no reason for them to behave like that, but Chris knew exactly why they were so bitter.

Avoiding staring at them was really difficult, because Chris was sitting on the far side of the table from them, facing directly towards the corner they occupied. Beside him, Nicky was having just as much trouble looking away, and he was side on. It was so hard to avoid eye contact . . .

'Who are you lookin' at, kid?' snapped Razor-cut.

Chris dropped his eyes back down to his half-eaten meal. From the edge of his vision, he saw his father stiffen. John Stephens had his back to the three men, so he hadn't really investigated them, even though he had been forced to listen to their loud conversation for the last twenty minutes. Now he turned in his seat to get a closer look, realising that the challenge was aimed their way.

There was a quiet determination in his father's face that was quite scary. Certainly, it was a lot more scary than the loud bragging of the three morons.

Fortunately, the three youths were distracted by the arrival of the first part of their meal. The waitress was the same one who was looking after Chris's table, and she wasn't the brightest woman Chris had ever met, so it was no surprise at all when Blond & Ugly told her she'd brought the wrong starter.

'I wanted the potato skins,' he whined aggressively.

The waitress oohed and aahed in the same flustered manner as the dim girl in *Friends*, flicking through her pad to see what she had written. Not that it would have mattered if she had found garlic bread written in the guy's handwriting. He said she was wrong – end of debate.

'Go and bring me what I ordered,' the guy snapped, louder than before. 'And bring us some more beers!'

The girl snatched up the plate and retreated quickly. The three guys laughed as she left, then started a noisy argument about whether to share the two starters she'd left behind. Chris felt Nicky reach over and brush his wrist.

'He did order the garlic bread,' Nicky whispered. 'He made all that fuss about having bacon on the potato skins, then changed his mind and ordered the bread. With extra cheese.'

Chris looked up. He was going to whisper back that this was information he could live without, when his eyes accidentally fixed on Razor-cut, who was slouched in his chair, eating onion rings with his fingers, spilling crumbs on his red and white shirt.

Razor-cut looked right back at him. His face twisted into an unpleasant snarl.

'Hey, kid, why are you gawping over here again?'

Chris started to drop his eyes, but Blond & Ugly had already snapped his head round to glare at Chris as well; even Tall & Giggling was beginning to turn in his seat. Chris hoped that they would offer a few more loud comments and then leave it at that.

'We were just looking at your shirts,' said Nicky. 'Have you heard the football results this afternoon?'

Great . . .

Chris groaned inside. Nicky had made the remark sound so innocent. Even so, the three men weren't that stupid. They could tell that Nicky was winding them up. Fiorentini had this knack for getting people to either really like him or want to bury his head in concrete.

The three lads looked like they belonged to the concrete group.

It was clear things were about to get ugly. Chris knew that he, his father and Nicky would be in the thick of it. The reason was simple, and fell into three parts. One, the three men were all wearing Southampton football shirts. Two, Chris and Nicky were wearing replica Oldcester United kit (although Nicky had covered his red and blue by buttoning up his jacket a few minutes before). Three, that afternoon United had thumped Southampton 6–1. And it hadn't been that close.

And now, thanks to Nicky (well, partly, anyway), Chris's premonition of trouble was about to come true.

⚽

John Stephens dropped his knife and fork on to his plate with a loud clatter as he twisted round in his seat. The rest of the restaurant seemed to fall silent in the aftermath of Razor-cut's shouted challenge.

Chris didn't move. A knot of fear tightened in his stomach. The tall guy with the dark hair leapt to his feet and turned round, his chair falling backwards. His fists were clenched tight. He looked very big and very angry, hanging over Chris's father like a thunder cloud. In fact, everything seemed to get darker for a moment.

That was the moment when Chris realised someone was brushing past him, moving rapidly through the narrow space behind his chair. The dark shadow he cast fell on the Southampton supporters. Blond & Ugly uttered a small squeak and banged his palm down on the table like a rabbit slapping the grass to warn his friends. Razor-cut tilted his head back, then back some more as he tried to look up at the new arrival.

The only one of the three still moving was the tall guy. He had raised one fist above his shoulder, as if he was going to slam it down on Chris's father from behind. Chris heard a sharp slapping sound, and then Tall Boy's mouth opened in a wide 'O'. At first he just looked surprised, but then his eyes wrinkled and closed as the pain bit hard. Just watching it made Chris wince.

The only way Chris could take in all of what was going on was to tilt his seat back. That was when he saw the giant standing behind Nicky's chair, leaning forward with his huge left hand clamped around Tall Boy's fist, squeezing hard. He must have caught it just as Tall Boy threw his punch at the back of John Stephens' head. Tall Boy's fingertips looked like tiny red worms trapped in the tight clamp of the giant's fist.

The big man held his right hand up, palm out and fingers splayed, as a warning to the others to stay out of it.

'Don't move,' he ordered them, in a voice that sounded a little like Arnold Schwarzenegger's, low and growling, and with a very strong accent. The two Southampton lads must have thought they'd come up against Conan or the Terminator as well, judging by the way they both took a step back and left their mate to take whatever punishment was coming next.

The giant turned his arm slightly, twisting Tall Boy's wrist so that he had to choose between falling back into his seat or having a broken hand. The guy cried out 'Let go!!' and 'Aaaah!!' a few times, but the giant wasn't convinced. Another turn of his arm, and Tall Boy was facing back towards his table, away from Chris and his father.

'Waitress!' called the giant, and the small young woman with the vacant eyes and the notepad scurried back.

'My friend says he *did* order the garlic bread. And he says forget the beer, just bring the bill. He has remembered they have a long drive home.'

Chris gaped in awe at the way the giant was defusing the situation. It helped that he was at least two metres high – what was that in old measures; six foot five, six six? – and that his arms were heavily muscled, bunched tight where he was gripping Tall Boy's fist.

But there was more to it than that. The giant had stepped in calmly, but with complete authority. His voice had been low and polite throughout – he hadn't made any wild threats or anything. The accent made it sound even stranger. He had pronounced 'remembered' more like 'rembert' and he made the word 'beer' sound like it had extra Es and a string of rolling Rs at the end. He had been in complete control of the situation from the moment he stepped in.

The three Southampton lads, on the other hand, were now completely dumbstruck, looking up at the giant with sheepish smiles on their faces. They had no idea how to cope with this sudden change in the odds. The giant gave Tall Boy's hand one last squeeze – there was an audible cracking noise – and slapped Razor-cut on the back so hard he almost pitched into his plate.

'Good to see you, boys,' said the giant. 'Your team was unlucky today. Perhaps you beat us down at The Dell, yes? Oh, by the way, could you keep the noise down a bit? I'm trying to have a meal. Don't forget to leave the waitress a big tip.'

And that was that. The giant walked back the way he had come, threading through the space between the tables until he reached a small booth on the side of the restaurant, where he disappeared. There was a small cheer from someone by the bar and a couple of other people clapped.

The Southampton lads ate their starters at world-record speed, then left about £30 on the table and scorch marks on the carpet as they went out through the door. Tall Boy was carrying his right hand in his left, as if it was still causing him pain. His face was puffy and red.

Chris and Nicky barely noticed them leave. Their attention was wholly fixed on the booth across the room, even though at first they couldn't see their rescuer at all. By leaning right back, Chris found he could get a glimpse of the giant's head over the top of the alcove's bench seats. He almost fell over until his father reached out with his foot and tipped his chair back forward.

'Do you realise who that was?' Chris gasped at last. It was the first time he had managed to speak since the incident started.

Nicky nodded, equally amazed. 'We have to go and meet him,' he said quickly, almost half out of his seat.

'Haven't you met him already?' asked Chris's father, trying to slow them down before they raced across the restaurant.

'No,' Chris replied without looking round. 'We've seen him at training once, but he was getting the guided tour of the ground and we were in the middle of some exercises, so he didn't come over.'

His father scratched his chin. 'So what's the hurry to meet him now? I mean, it's not like he's the first Oldcester United player you've ever met.'

'This is different,' said Nicky, as if that explained everything. 'Come on, Mr Stephens, we have to go and say thanks, don't we?'

Mr Stephens opened his mouth as if he was going to object, but then said nothing in reply. He had spent too many Saturdays with Nicky not to recognise when Nicky wouldn't take no for an answer.

In any case, just as Nicky finished speaking, the waitress came over, bringing them three fresh drinks and a huge dessert that came in a vast bowl, with enough cream and fruit and ice cream to feed the entire restaurant. She looked very pleased with herself, and that was before she took the £30 from the other table.

'The gentleman in the alcove paid for this. He says if it's too much and you'd like to share it, would you care to join him?'

Chris and Nicky took off from their seats like rockets on 5 November.

Two

Eating in the Harvester on the western ring road was a new part of the Saturday home-match ritual. Apart from that, the day had been the same as any other home-match Saturday, up to the point when Razor-cut had glared back at Chris. Well, true, 6–1 thrashings were pretty rare (at least with Oldcester on the right end of the result), but win or lose, Chris, his father and Nicky had been following the same routine for many years.

Now, of course, the day would be remembered as the occasion when they had dinner with Pavel Davidov, Oldcester's new centre back, and the hero of Star Park after just half a dozen games. Chris could hardly wait for school on Monday, so that he and Nicky could brag about it to the others.

It was proving to be a good year for bragging. During the summer, Chris and Nicky had been accepted on to the youth team at Oldcester United, an ambition they had shared for years. After several successful seasons with their school team and a year in the local youth league, they had come through the trials at the second attempt and had been training at Star Park since September.

What made their success even better was that both Chris and Nicky were fanatical United supporters.

To be honest, that made them a bit of a rarity, even in Oldcester. United weren't one of the big Premiership outfits – in fact, even the visit of Southampton had felt like the arrival of a big-city team. Plenty of the other kids at school supported Manchester United, Spurs or Forest ... there was even an Ipswich fan, although she didn't count.

However, that winter, being one of the red and blues was about the coolest thing on the planet. United were third in the

Premiership, on the back of an eight-game unbeaten run, trailing Manchester United and Chelsea by just a point and with a better goal difference. This was the best start to the season anyone could remember, even a Statto like Nicky. OK, in their hearts United's red and blue army knew the bubble would probably burst in the new year, and they'd end up squabbling around in mid-table with Spurs, Coventry and Everton, but for now they were riding high and making the most of every moment as the surprise team of the season.

It seemed almost incredible now that Oldcester had recently spent a season in the First Division. Not that it had made much difference to Chris, Nicky and Chris's dad – they turned up to almost every home game and a few away fixtures, even when those games had taken them to Norwich or Luton, and not Old Trafford or White Hart Lane. It was a popular saying locally that Oldcester supporters had red arteries and blue veins.

Every club, large or small, has its die-hard supporters, and in Oldcester you could die very hard indeed as a United fan. One FA Cup win in 100 years – and that long before Chris was born – wasn't much success to crow about. It didn't matter. If you supported Liverpool or Arsenal or even Leeds, you expected success. You had all that history weighing you down. As a supporter of Oldcester United, you got used to the fact that you couldn't talk about the season you won the double, or back-to-back European trophies . . . Instead you had to settle for single games that lit up the memory like neon. An away win at Anfield; a comeback draw against the Gunners.

Every United supporter had their favourite. For Chris, it was the first game he ever saw – a thrilling 1–1 draw against Coventry in the Cup. From that moment on, he was hooked. He and his father had been season-ticket holders for years, and Nicky joined them soon after, sitting with them in the Easter Road Stand even when members of his own family were elsewhere in the ground. The ritual never changed much.

On the way out of Star Park, listening to the buzz from the crowd as they streamed along Easter Road back towards the city centre, it was easy to imagine some other young kid among the 26,500 supporters, perhaps visiting the stadium for the first time, who would always remember the day Oldcester

United went third in the table after they turned on the style against Southampton.

It was days like that which made being a football supporter the best thing in the world. For Chris and his fellow United supporters, they were all the better for being rare. It made you appreciate them more.

But that winter was even better. That run of eight games without a defeat had started with two away draws. The last six games had all been wins, and only a single goal had been conceded. Each week it seemed like there was a different Man of the Match, but word was starting to creep round the city that the big difference in the team was a chance signing manager Phil Parkes had made in the autumn. No-one had expected the signing, since Oldcester weren't the kind of club to splash out a couple of million too often, but Parkes had signed the centre back from a hard-up Russian team for just under £1.5 million. Oldcester's defence had never been that solid in the past. Now, suddenly, no-one seemed to be able to find a way through.

Up close, sitting across the table from the gigantic frame of Pavel Davidov, it was easy to see why.

'How big is he?' asked Fuller.

That was the fifth time Chris had been asked the same question in the last hour, and the second time by Fuller. The reflected glory of having sat at the same table as United's new signing was wearing a little thin.

'Two point oh-four metres,' replied Chris, remembering the note in the programme.

That number meant nothing to Fuller, who stood with his arm stretched up and his hand levelled flat, as if he was accurately depicting the chosen height.

'Bigger,' sighed Chris, walking away from the building towards the school gates. He turned and watched Fuller pause at the end of the wall, trying to puzzle out where two and a bit metres might come up to. The odds were that Fuller didn't know that a metre was 39 inches, and it was a racing certainty that he couldn't multiply that by two and then convert the answer into feet and inches. Various other members of the small group attached to Chris were making helpful suggestions as if they were the audience on an ITV game show.

'Bigger than Flea, then?' Fuller asked, ignoring the chorus of 'Higher, higher!' and 'Lower, lower!' from other members of the group. Everyone fancied they could do Bruce impressions.

Chris came to a stop and closed his eyes, wondering if he was getting a headache. They had already been round this once before. It was the last day of term, and school had just finished at lunchtime. They could be out enjoying that fact. Instead . . .

Chris made the mental comparison once again. 'Flea' was the PE master at Spirebrook Comprehensive, and a big man, as anyone who had ever played rugby against him would confirm. The sports teacher was frighteningly large when he came charging towards you, which had improved the speed of the school rugby team's passing no end.

But a lot of Flea's size went sideways. His shoulders were massive and his chest was the same size as one of the big rubbish bins parked outside the dining hall.

Pavel Davidov was different. He wasn't fat or heavy-built or anything like that, he was just HUGE. It was as if someone had taken a regular human being and scaled them up all round. Not only was he tall, but he had huge, powerful arms and vast hands, not to mention legs that looked like the trunks of small oak trees. The word was that the club had kit specially made for him. And yet all that size was more or less in proportion.

Which meant that on his own he didn't look that big, even out on the pitch. But there had been a moment in the game on Saturday when he had put a consoling arm round Matt Le Tissier, and it seemed as though Matt was about ten and talking to his dad.

Le Tissier had become the first player to score against the new-look United defence, a typical class strike that had seen him twice flick the ball over smaller defenders. He had seen Davidov bearing down on him, and that – according to the crowd – was why he had taken a shot on goal, and not because he saw the keeper off his line.

Chris remembered the Russian's shadow passing over him in the restaurant. It had been like an eclipse.

While Fuller continued to try and measure Davidov's height (or what he imagined it to be) against the wall of the upper-school bog, the rest of the gang started walking towards the gates again. The conversation returned to the important story of Saturday's match and how the Russian had scared the jelly out of the Southampton supporters.

'I didn't think you got trouble at matches these days,' said Jazz with a sad note in his voice. He had been trying hard to persuade his father to let him go to a few games each season, and football violence was the reason his father trotted out each time he said no.

'This wasn't at the ground, dummy,' snapped Griff, the captain of the school's senior team, and therefore an expert on everything.

Chris gave Jazz a more measured reply. 'Those three were an exception,' he explained. 'They had had too much to drink and they thought they could make a fuss in the restaurant and no-one would stop them. It was just bad luck we were in their way.'

'It was dumb luck to find three Southampton supporters in the same place,' said Nicky, smirking. 'I didn't think they had enough fans to have a hooligan minority.' A few of the others laughed, sharing Nicky's instant prejudice against the supporters of a team which often shared United's fight against relegation.

'I don't know that it was bad luck after all,' Jazz said, sounding really fed up. 'At least you got to meet Pavel Davidov.'

Some of the others agreed. Chris was still on the new subject, however.

'It's not about them supporting Southampton,' he explained. 'Those idiots could have been from London, Manchester . . . or Doncaster, remember?' A couple of the others nodded, remembering the worst night at Star Park for years, a Coca-Cola tie against Doncaster which had turned ugly. The away fans had grown very bitter over a couple of refereeing decisions and tore up some seats. Nicky had said at the time (he and Chris were in their usual place) that he couldn't see why Doncaster fans should ever get upset about losing, since they must be used to it. Eventually, it came out that most of the troublemakers were from a different city entirely, who had driven down to watch the game when their team's tie was postponed.

'Ah,' Nicky had said at the time, 'that explains it.'

In the world according to Nicky Fiorentini, maybe it did make sense, but Chris couldn't understand why anyone could go mental about a game of football. If losing a match was all it took, Star Park would have been razed to the ground long ago.

This was an old subject for discussion among the Spirebrook Comp football clique. Interestingly, it was the new recruit, Robert James, a lad two years younger than Chris and Nicky, who managed to put a new spin on the proceedings at about the moment they passed through the gates.

'It's all about money,' he said, and his voice managed to find its way through gaps in the conversation so that everyone heard him.

'What was that?' asked Griff.

'Money,' James repeated. 'There's so much money in the game now, it's changing everything. Think about it; you pay twenty-five quid for a ticket, plus whatever it costs to get to the game, then you watch your team play like a bunch of wallies and get thumped six-one. People just get frustrated.'

Robert James had only started at Spirebrook in the summer, but he had already overtaken Nicky's record for causing arguments. Those two sentences managed to get three different debates going. Griff shouted at James about all the trouble there had been back in the seventies, long before the Premiership and all the money that had brought; Nicky and Jazz argued about how much trouble there was at football grounds, and whether fans were more likely to cause trouble in the pubs later; and Mac, who'd read somewhere that most football hooligans were people with well-paid jobs and no real interest in football, was trying to explain this to Fuller, who blamed the Tory government, the tabloids and the influx of foreign players who couldn't speak English, without even trying to explain the hows and whys of anything he said.

Chris flitted in and out of a couple of the arguments, but his heart wasn't really in any of them. He was still remembering the buzz he had got out of sitting opposite Davidov, talking about football and Oldcester and what it was like to live in a new country. The defender's family were due to arrive from Moscow any day. He was just your ordinary giant.

Chris had never really thought about the money side of football before, even though his whole life was focused on becoming a professional footballer for United. When his mates talked about how much money he'd earn as a pro, Chris just laughed.

Sure, he knew about transfer fees, the sky-high wages the top players earned and how much the season tickets his father bought each season cost. He'd read about the gambling that took place in places like Hong Kong, and how matches were sometimes rigged. It was only a few months ago that he had met up with someone who had been involved in that kind of stuff, or at least that was what Chris had been told.

But Chris had never really considered the way money and football came together, and what effect the former had on the latter. Little did he realise, as he and the guys talked about the incident in the Harvester, that he was just a few days away from a crash course.

Three

After leaving school, Chris, Nicky and Russell Jones set off towards the city, catching the bus from the stop on the main road opposite Chris's turning. Their plan was to spend a couple of hours in the city before making their way over to Star Park for the last practice session before Christmas.

It meant they'd been carrying their kit around with them all day, but that didn't matter. It was a cool afternoon, but there was some weak sunshine to make everything look a little brighter. Chris and Russell were looking forward to enjoying a few hours larking around before they made their way over the river for what would probably be a relaxed last session before the holidays.

The youth team normally trained at the back end of the week, but this special Monday session had been arranged because Christmas Day was on a Thursday, and Sean Priest, the youth team manager, had told the lads he wanted to have them together one last time before they all stuffed themselves with Christmas pud.

'I hear they come up with some other stuff as well,' said Russell. Chris had heard the same stories from players who had been in the squad in previous years. Sean Priest never missed a chance to spring a surprise.

As they made their way into town, Chris realised Nicky was in a pretty grumpy mood for some reason he couldn't work out. Normally, Nicky took charge when they made one of these rare expeditions to the city centre, since he was often the only one who had any money. However, after buying the new Dodgy album in Virgin, which he promised to loan to Chris in the new year, Nicky didn't seem to be that interested in wandering round, so they settled for a burger and Coke at Mad Mick's.

'What's his problem?' asked Russell, while he and Chris queued. Nicky had given them his money while he went off to find a table. They could see him stalking through the open-air seating like a bear with a sore head.

'I've no idea,' sighed Chris, although he was pretty sure they'd find out soon enough. Nicky never kept his moods a secret for long. Unfortunately, this particular sulk distracted Chris just long enough for him to make a small error.

'Maybe he's found out he's not getting a new mountain bike for Christmas after all,' Chris said, not even looking at Russell as he made the joke. A half-second too late, he realised what he'd just said, and to who. 'Oh, I . . . uh . . .' he stumbled.

'It's OK, Chris,' Russell said, grinning, as he watched Chris search for a neat way to apologise. Chris smiled back weakly. The gulf between the sort of Christmas Nicky could expect – with his huge family of fully-employed relations indulging his every whim – and the kind Russell might enjoy was vast. Russell had a father who only worked about eight days a year, a mother who treated trips to Tesco as if they were major expeditions to find life on Mars and a younger brother and sister who probably were from Mars. None of this lot were likely to buy Russell anything over the holiday. In the Jones house, they probably didn't have turkey, just some leftover ham with feathers stuck in it to make it look seasonal.

There was another brother, but any goodies he put under the Christmas tree would have been pinched from some store or warehouse, along with the tree. The idea of Mick Jones slipping down your chimney singing 'Ho, ho, ho!' wasn't something Chris wanted to think about.

'I'm sorry,' Chris said at last.

Russell shrugged to show that he wasn't offended. 'Forget it,' he told his team mate. 'Nicky says he's already seen a new forty-speed, all-singing, all-dancing, make-the-tea mountain bike in the garage. You know what he's like. If his Christmas present is still a surprise in October, it's a miracle.'

Chris grinned, relieved that Russell was so cool about this stuff. He had also remembered Russell and Nicky had some plan whereby Russell got Nicky's 'old' bike, a 'pile of junk' that was all of two years old.

'Any idea what you're getting?'

Chris shook his head. Last year, his father had splashed out on a new Macintosh computer they could barely afford, making use of his employee discount at the computer warehouse. Chris had already been told he couldn't expect anything quite so grand this year.

In fact, he had already resigned himself to this Christmas being a bit of a disappointment. When his father landed the new job, he made a trade-off to get every other Saturday afternoon off, allowing him to carry on taking Chris and Nicky to see United. This meant he covered a whole load of late openings and stuff like that. With the store opening until 10pm on Christmas Eve, this meant Chris wouldn't see too much of his dad until Christmas Day itself.

Because of this, Mr Stephens had arranged for Chris to spend the next few days down in London with an aunt he hadn't seen for three years. John Stephens was going to drive down late Christmas Eve to join them. They had tickets for United's game against Chelsea at Stamford Bridge on the Saturday, after which they were going to head back to Oldcester. Chris's dad would be back at work on Monday.

Chris had told his school mates about this as soon as it had been decided. Although the visit to the Bridge was cool – and even cooler now that it would be a top-of-the-table clash – most of them thought that being forced to spend two days with some aged and half-forgotten aunt was a pretty poor way to start the holiday.

'My dad doesn't want me alone in the house,' Chris had explained. 'He'll be working until gone nine both nights.'

'So why not camp out round at Nicky's?' they'd asked.

Which was a fair question, given that Chris spent half his life at the Fiorentini mansion anyway, and one more mouth to feed at the dinner table wouldn't stretch Mrs Fiorentini even a little. She always cooked enough for double the number of people she expected to sit down.

As he and Russell queued at Mad Mick's, which was universally recognised as the best place to eat in the city, Chris wondered if this business with Christmas was why Nicky was in a mood. Sure enough, once they had purchased their food and made their way to the table Nicky had nabbed, it didn't take long for the truth to come out.

First off, though, they had to endure the tail end of a row between Nicky and a man of about 40 who was wearing a heavy dark coat and carrying a bulky black suitcase. Nicky was sitting very stubbornly in a chair, arms folded, glaring back at the man. The argument appeared to be about the kit bags occupying two other seats.

Chris handed over Nicky's food, trying hard not to get involved. It didn't work. As soon as he pulled back the heavy metal chair his bag was parked on, the row flared up again.

'See, just like I told you,' Nicky snapped at the man. 'These are my mates. Three of us; three chairs. OK?'

Chris caught a flash of brilliant blue eyes as the guy glared at him. The man was wearing a baseball cap pulled down tight on his head, and a scarf muffled his mouth. Between the two, the eyes flashed out like searchlights. Chris turned away. He heard the man move off between the crowded chairs.

The Wanderers was a popular place even on a quiet day, being right in the middle of town and surrounded by cafes, restaurants and delis. Right now, it was jampacked with people finishing off their Christmas shopping and taking a few minutes out to get a bite to eat. When Chris next took a peek, the guy was standing some distance off, with a sandwich in his mouth.

As he watched, Chris saw the guy open the case on his knee and pull out what looked like a large black book or a carrying case for binoculars. The guy tipped this on end and pulled something out. Chris wasn't sure, but it looked metallic. His curiosity would have kept him focused on the juggling act that followed as the man tried to eat, replace the leather wallet in his case and stand on one leg. However, Nicky was trying to attract his attention.

'Which is my burger?' Fiorentini demanded. Chris pointed at none of them; it hardly mattered, given that they were all the same. All Mad Mick's burgers turned out identically, no matter what people asked him for.

Nicky grabbed his burger without additional comment. Realising that Chris was staring past him, Nicky turned to take a quick look at the man as well. He was moving further away now, rustling and clattering as he pressed between the closely packed chairs.

'Moron,' muttered Nicky. He faced Chris. 'Did you hear him? He talked funnier than that bloke on the TV; the one who does that cooking quiz thing. Lloyd thingy.'

'*Masterchef*,' Chris offered. Then he added 'Grossman' in case there was any chance Nicky had the programme and the presenter mixed up.

'Yeah, that's him,' Nicky agreed.

Chris was all for changing the subject, and looked up at Russell for help. Which is what he got, sort of.

'When do you leave to go down to your aunt's?' Jones asked between mouthfuls of burger, Coke and fries.

'I'm getting the nine forty-five train,' Chris replied. He saw Nicky look up, with a bored expression creeping on to his face in place of the sullen pout.

'What time will you get there?'

'About one, or half past,' Chris answered, even more quietly.

Russell nodded as if this information was really fascinating, and then packed his mouth with another load, chewing heavily. Chris glanced across at Nicky again, and saw Fiorentini push his fringe back from his eyes. His brows were knotted in a deep frown, as they always were when he was thinking.

'Does the train go through Hendon?' he asked, abruptly.

Chris couldn't remember. He wondered why Nicky was interested.

'That's where Paulo lives,' Fiorentini disclosed, as if that explained his interest. Paulo was one of his two cousins who played in the Icis League. Paulo fancied himself as a bit of a David Ginola, but the only time Chris had seen him play he'd made an ass of himself trying to impress the United coaching staff. Both cousins were regular visitors at Nicky's house, where the other cousin's girlfriend was now in residence while she studied at Oldcester University.

'It's in north London,' Nicky continued, which made even Russell look up, since it was rare for Nicky to be able to find Oldcester on a map, never mind know the location of somewhere as exotic as Hendon.

Chris explained again that he wasn't sure where the train passed through, but it didn't stop in Hendon, or anywhere south of Bedford, as far as he knew. Nicky asked where Bedford was.

'I still don't know why you're bothering,' Russell said, thinking out loud more than anything.

'My dad doesn't want me at home alone on Christmas Eve,' Chris explained wearily, for what seemed like the thousandth time. Russell nodded to show that he knew that, licked a glob of mayonnaise from his lip, and broke in before Chris trotted out the rest of the story.

'Why couldn't you just go round to Nicky's?' he asked.

Chris took a deep breath, and was on the point of answering the question when he saw that Nicky was looking directly at him. His brain was trying to remind his mouth that his father wanted to see his sister anyway, and they had tickets for the Chelsea game, and it just made sense to spend Christmas with Aunt Helen. Instead, no sound came out. For the first time, Chris found himself asking just why he *really* wasn't going to hang out at Nicky's over the holiday.

And, he realised, it was because Nicky hadn't asked him.

The two of them stared at each other for a moment, exchanging the kind of silent messages that passed between them on the pitch, when they always seemed to know what the other was thinking. Russell lifted his head up, mid-bite, looking from one to the other.

'I would have asked . . .' Nicky began.

'It's OK, you know,' Chris said at the same moment, and they continued to talk across each other for a few seconds. Nicky's voice became slightly louder as he spilled out just what was bugging him, and Chris slowly increased the volume of his own speech, just to make himself heard.

Russell listened, the burger poised at his lips, and took it all in. At the end, all he could be sure of was that maybe his family was easier to deal with after all.

Four

'Nicky's place is going to be packed,' Chris explained. 'There's all his family, plus his Uncle Fabian. Then both his cousins are coming up from London; plus there's the other cousin who works in TV – she's staying; plus there's his cousin's girlfriend, and now some other cousin who's coming over from Italy.'

Chris was counting them all off on his fingers, trying to make sure he kept track of the whole Fiorentini clan. It was easy to mislay at least a few cousins. It was so hard to keep track of them all. Some were important cousins – the Premier League types. Then there were Nationwide cousins, and GM Conference cousins and several divisions of Icis League cousins . . .

'That's why Nicky is so ticked off. It was the final straw, you know, in the Battle of the Bedroom.'

He was talking very loudly to make himself heard over the music blaring out of a shop doorway. All the way along Oxford Street, they had been assaulted by noise. Music, traffic and the constant barrage of people talking and shouting. The din was astonishing. London made Oldcester city centre seem like a country village on a Sunday afternoon. It never looked this bad on *EastEnders* or *Thief Takers* . . .

Aunt Helen looked round, with an expression on her face that at first made Chris wonder if he'd lost her somewhere back at the beginning of the list. Then he realised that she might not be completely up to date with the territorial battles in the Fiorentini household.

'The two girls living there at the moment – aside from Nicky's sisters, that is – share a room. It's smaller than Nicky's, so they have been on at him to swap. Now this Alexandra girl is arriving from Italy, the pressure on Nicky is growing. He doesn't think he'll be able to hold out much longer.'

Aunt Helen nodded, but Chris could tell that she didn't

really get it. The Stephens were a small family. Helen had never married, and she didn't have any kids. Aside from some distant great-aunts, she was about all Chris and his father had. Chris couldn't imagine there had ever been a time when his father and Helen had fought about space the way the Fiorentinis did.

'Anyway, that's why I couldn't go to stay with him,' Chris added.

Helen nodded to show she was still listening, but her attention was fixed on a shop window, and she slid gracefully across the pavement to take a closer look. Chris, trying to follow her, became tangled up instantly in a whole gang of other shoppers. He tried to swerve around a woman in a heavy woollen coat, but she still thumped into him with her arm. Chris turned to apologise, but she had already vanished, swallowed up by the crowd.

A tall man with a goatee beard and a newspaper under his arm came on as substitute, appearing out of nowhere to block Chris's path to the window. If guys like him ever played football, Chris decided, he'd never score again. Luckily, Oldcester United Youth Team almost never played fixtures on Oxford Street in the last few days before Christmas.

Chris just couldn't believe how crowded, noisy and chaotic it was. He'd been to London perhaps twice in his life. Sure, it had been pretty busy then, even compared to Oldcester's busiest days, but today was manic! Aunt Helen had picked him up at the station, and told him that they'd walk down Tottenham Court Road and check out the last-minute bargains on Oxford Street.

If there were any bargains to be had, Chris decided, they came at too high a price. He'd been up against some pretty rough defenders in his career, but nothing to compare with the sweepers who patrolled the streets of London. One smartly dressed young woman cracked him hard on the elbow with her umbrella, and even before Chris managed to yell 'Ow!', a suit with a mobile phone glued to his ear clattered into him from behind, a definite bookable challenge if ever there was one.

Aunt Helen, though, swooped and swerved smoothly through the traffic like she was skating on ice. She never seemed to be looking where she was going, but no-one so much as grazed her royal blue coat or threatened the carrier bags she clutched. One of the bags, Chris knew, contained a hideous glass ornament she had just bought for his father. They had a collection of similar ornaments at home, safely under lock and key. If anything deserved to be on the wrong end of a crunching tackle . . .

Chris tried again to fight his way to the shop window, and wondered if he could get Aunt Helen to show him a few moves. If she could teach him to sidestep London crowds, he reckoned he'd never be tackled by a defender again.

'What do you think?' she asked as he arrived at her elbow.

Chris peered through the window. They were looking into some kind of charity shop. Beyond the display, Chris could see the kind of crowd United would consider a good gate at Star Park, all packed into one store. Chris cast his eye over what was attracting them.

The display featured dozens of Christmas novelties. There was a glow-in-the-dark carol singer made of plastic, which played 'Hark The Herald Angels Sing', according to the sign beside it. Chris had seen something similar being sold by a roadside vendor about 50 metres and 5000 people back, only his was half the price and played a squeaky digital version of a tune Chris didn't even recognise.

There were Santa bow-ties which lit up and played tunes; miniature Christmas trees with LED lights which played tunes; bright orange Rudolph reindeer with noses that lit up (and probably played tunes). If it looked Christmassy, and you could stick a bulb and a sound chip in it, this shop had it.

'A few of those would brighten up the flat, don't you think?'

Chris winced at the idea of even one of them, but Aunt Helen was already on her way to the shop door.

'I'll wait here, Aunt Helen!' he called. 'It looks a bit crowded in there.'

'OK, dear!' his aunt called back. 'Don't wander off!'

Chris smiled reassuringly and watched as she walked briskly through the doorway and into the depths of the store without making the slightest physical contact with anyone, not even the swarthy, bearded gentleman who seemed to try and bump into her, but who missed when she pivoted on her he[illegible] and changed direction.

Chris turned away from the window and its flashing lights, trying to find a space he could call his own. It was laughable to complain about the store being crowded, of course, since the pavement was jammed solid too. Every two seconds, Chris was jostled as shoppers inspected the window. 'Ho, ho, ho!' Chris grinned at a couple. They weren't amused.

He watched as a bus crawled past along the road. He and Aunt Helen had overtaken it about five minutes before as they had turned into Oxford Street. Chris had almost enjoyed Tottenham Court Road, which was two solid rows of discount electrical stores on each side of the street, with every kind of computer, TV, hi-fi, camera and battery-driven gadget on the planet. Chris liked the look of a pocket-sized organiser which could plug into the back of the Mac at home. It would be almost the same as having a laptop.

The decent models were around £60. Maybe next year.

Chris heard the charity shop's door open. The swarthy guy came out, looking both ways as if he had any chance of seeing more than a metre in any direction. He had his arms folded across the front of his coat, a dark, dirty, threadbare affair. He moved off, trying to dart into the spaces between people Aunt Helen found so easily, but he didn't have half her style.

Something bothered Chris about the situation right away. He felt a small warning twinge creep up the back of his neck, but the guy vanished into the crowd so quickly there was nothing he could do. Chris lifted himself on to his toes to look over the heads around him, and saw the man crossing the road behind the bus. Seconds after, he lost him.

The idea popped into Chris's mind that the guy might have been a pickpocket; that he might have been trying to steal something from Aunt Helen's bag. He turned to look in through the window again. At once he saw her, paying for some of the garish novelties, her purse safe in her hand. Chris breathed a sigh of relief.

He was letting his imagination get on top of him. Even so, he couldn't help rising up on the balls of his feet again, trying to get another glimpse of the dark-skinned man.

At once he felt his heart jump. Fractionally before he heard the yell, Chris caught sight of a closely cropped blond head on the far side of the road, towering above the people around it. His view was obstructed by people close by, but Chris was at the point of realising that he knew that head when a woman yelled out:

'Hey! Stop that man!!! He's stolen my bag!!!'

She had a high, piercing voice which could probably carry for miles on a still day, which was one reason why Chris caught the words so clearly. It helped that he was looking in roughly the direction the words had come from, across the road and down a little towards Bond Street. Amazingly, no-one else heard a thing, as far as Chris could tell. A few heads turned, but otherwise there was hardly any reaction in the crowd. Perhaps they thought it was a car alarm, or some other noise they were supposed to ignore.

Chris took an instinctive step forward, away from the window. Before he even realised he was moving, he was at the kerb. He felt his body tense, as if he was waiting for one of Nicky's fast, flat crosses to come flying across in front of him.

The roadway itself was one of the least crowded parts of Oxford Street, although none of the unlucky passengers in the near-stationary buses and taxis would have agreed. However, compared to the pavement, the road was relatively open, which made it the best place to be if you were a man in a hurry. Shoppers were crossing from one side of Oxford Street to the other, searching for an elusive bargain or just hurrying to get away from all the madness around them. One guy, though, was making a really determined break for freedom.

The swarthy guy, the guy who had recently left the shop where Aunt Helen was still waiting for her credit card and receipt. Mr Dark & Unshaven.

He was moving at a full sprint, racing up the centre of the road, between the two lines of creeping traffic. His coat was flapping around his legs. He still had one hand close to his chest, which was slowing him down, and Chris saw he was clutching something against his ragged check shirt. It was some kind of large leather bag with a shoulder strap, not much different to the one in which Aunt Helen carried her purse (along with a ton of other vital equipment . . .).

The hairs on Chris's neck stood up a little taller, and the small warning bell in his head called for his attention even more strongly than before. He hovered on the edge of the road as the man came closer, running for all he was worth, his eyes wide and his long black hair blown back around his scalp

Then Chris caught sight of a large shadow coming up the kerb on the other side of the road, clearing a space through the thick press of people by sheer physical presence alone.

Immediately, Chris knew what he had to do.

Dark & Unshaven's line up the middle of Oxford Street might have been the quickest route, but it was also very predictable. Chris stepped off the kerb behind a taxi that was crawling along just fast enough to reach Hyde Park by New Year's Day. As he crossed behind its boot, he ducked down so that the vehicle screened him from view. Watching through the rear window, Chris saw the swarthy guy coming closer, running towards the driver's side of the cab. He had turned his head to the left, nervously keeping a very close eye on the far side of the road.

Chris caught his target from the blind side as he came up. The man wasn't that big, and all Chris needed to do was give him a little shove. With his arm up to hold the bag, the guy was unprotected on his right and off balance.

Even so, Chris was amazed at how Dark & Unshaven took off. He clipped the wing of a dark blue car with his left knee and went up in the air like an acrobat or a stunt man, arms, legs and coat tails flailing. He landed on the bonnet, rolled over and disappeared on the far side.

'Ooops!' Chris muttered, holding up his hands as if he was admitting his guilt to a ref. 'Sorry.'

There was a lot of apologising going on on the far side of the road too. People dodged clear as someone pushed through the crowd. A large shadow closed down the last few metres to where the thief had fallen. Chris felt his heartbeat quicken, and he ran swiftly out from behind the cab, spinning around the dark blue Sierra. The driver yelled at him as he went past, having just recovered from seeing someone perform a cartwheel across his windshield.

The black-haired man was sitting against a lamppost on the side of the road, looking as if he had suddenly become very tired and needed to take a rest. His eyes were popping out, and his skin seemed to have become paler. There was a small mark on the lower part of his cheek where he had thumped into something. His coat had fallen wide open and the dark bag Chris had glimpsed was lying in the gutter under his leg.

A large hand fixed itself on the guy's collar and hauled him upright. He managed to look even more surprised. The hand tightened its grip and lifted him higher, so that his feet were off the floor.

'Where is lady's bag?' snarled a thick, angry voice.

Chris took a last step forward. 'It's OK, Pavel, it's here,' he said, and he bent down to pick up the fallen bag. When he stood up, smiling, he found that the dark man wasn't the only one whose face was frozen in shock.

⚽

'Hello again,' said Chris, grinning. 'Remember me?'

It was clear Pavel Davidov knew perfectly well who Chris was. On the other hand, he was having a great deal of difficulty believing what he was seeing. Finally, he managed a few words.

'You are boy from restaurant . . . Chris, yes?'

Pavel managed to make his name sound like it was spelt 'Krees', but Chris didn't care. He was just happy he'd been remembered.

'That's right.' Chris beamed proudly.

'What are you doing here?' Davidov said, still sounding completely off balance.

'I'm with my aunt,' Chris said, making a useless gesture back towards the shop behind him, as if that could possibly identify who he was with.

Pavel's head tilted as he followed the direction in which Chris was pointing. His mouth opened, but nothing came out. In fact, the only one with anything to say at that point was the dark man dangling in Pavel's grip.

'I'm choking!'

In fairness, his collar did look a little tight, but all he achieved by opening his trap was to attract Pavel's attention. The big Russian stared at him, his brows lowering over his pale blue eyes as he glared at the small man in his fist.

'I shouldn't have been moved, you know . . .' the smaller man squawked. 'After a fall like that, I could have concussion, or broken bones.'

'We can soon check you for broken bones,' snarled Davidov, lifting his free hand as if he was going to conduct the examination by pounding on the guy's ribs one by one. The effect was slightly spoilt by the fact that Pavel had a woman's handbag in his left hand. It was the same kind as the one Chris held; a black leather bag with thick handles, rather like Aunt Helen's. There seemed to be a lot of them about.

Davidov turned his large, heavily boned head to look back along the street in the direction he had come from. 'He took bag from woman,' he explained, gesturing back along the street with his head. 'He bumped into her, snatched bag, then dropped this one.' He lifted his left hand slightly to show the item he was talking about.

'A simple mix-up!' the man cried desperately, his voice slightly choked by the tight grasp of Pavel's fist. 'I dropped my bag and took the other woman's by mistake.'

'Shuttup,' snapped Davidov.

'I think he took the bag you've got from someone in the shop over there,' Chris explained, repeating the gesture he had made earlier. Pavel looked as if he was getting used to it.

'It's my sister's!' the bag thief insisted.

'Shuttup,' Pavel and Chris said together. Chris liked the way it sounded in the Russian's thick, solid accent, as if it was all one word.

'We should try to get these back to the right people,' Chris said. Pavel was still staring up the street, with the thief in one hand and the bag in the other. The pale eyes narrowed as if the Russian could see something heading their way that he didn't like the look of. He looked at the bag, hesitated, then turned to Chris.

'You know who this belong to?' he asked.

Chris knew at once that there was something not quite right. He smiled back at the Russian, trying to gather his thoughts.

'Not definitely, no, but –'

'Take it, and give me other one,' Davidov said quickly, and he tossed over the bag he was holding. Chris caught it, then held out the one the thief had been carrying when Chris tackled him. Davidov looked at it as if the bag contained poison, then slowly lowered the dark man to the ground and released his grip. He took the bag in his right hand.

Chris remained where he was, wondering what was going on. The bag snatcher didn't look any less confused. Chris saw him sizing up possible escape routes.

'Is anything –' Chris began.

'Go quickly,' Davidov said, and there was a slight catch in his voice. Chris turned to look up Oxford Street, in the direction from which Davidov had come. A young blonde woman was pushing through the crowd (which had stopped to watch the show, but was now slowly drifting away). Immediately behind her were two men. The first was a small guy with an odd mark on his cheekbone, an earring large enough to qualify him as a Bajoran on *Star Trek* and thin, greasy hair swept back from his forehead; the second was an ugly bruiser with a thick lip, bushy eyebrows and a set of clothes that were several sizes too small for him. A hot-air balloon might just have covered him, but it would have been tight.

Chris stepped away, but only slowly. His curiosity was piqued. It didn't help that the bag thief seemed to have developed a pressing need to disappear back on to the floor, behind the litter bin, as the newcomers approached.

Davidov's head snapped round, away from the woman and the two men, and directly towards Chris. 'Go now!' he shouted commandingly, his voice a deep, hard sound.

Chris took several steps back without even realising he was walking. His father had never managed to get him to move that quickly, despite years of practice. There was something about the way Pavel spoke that made Chris do exactly what the big man said.

As he backed away between the taxis and buses, he was still facing the pavement. He saw the woman run the last few steps towards Davidov, leaving the two men trailing behind her. He saw Pavel holding out the bag with a weak smile.

But just before that, he saw the big man dig his hand into the bag and pull out something dark. His hand went behind his back, out of the woman's sight. Chris saw the street thief look up and his eyes widen. What was this?

A taxi honked its horn at him, and Chris spun round to look where he was going. At once, he saw Aunt Helen in the shop doorway. She had her arm around an elderly woman in a smart green check coat, and they both looked quite distressed. When Helen caught sight of Chris, her anxiety vanished. Chris knew she had been worried when she stepped from the shop and couldn't see him.

'Chris . . . where have you been?' she asked. Without waiting for an answer, she added: 'This woman had her bag taken; some man just –'

'Is this it?' asked Chris, holding up the bag.

The old woman looked up and her expression became one of great relief and joy. A quick check proved that it was indeed her bag, snatched from the floor while she had been looking through the gifts on sale. Everything that was supposed to be inside was still there. The thief hadn't taken anything.

'Thank you, young man, thank you!' she cried. There were still tears pouring from her eyes, but they were tears of relief now. She fumbled with her purse. 'Let me give you something as a reward.'

At the same time, Aunt Helen demanded to know how Chris had managed to recover the bag. Chris started to argue that the old woman didn't owe him any reward, as a prelude to explaining to both her and Aunt Helen what had happened, when he remembered that the woman *really* didn't owe him anything. Pavel had rescued her bag, while Chris had –

He turned round and looked back across the street so that he could indicate the rest of the people involved. But there was no-one there. The flow of people was much like it had been before, a solid press of disinterested shapes in winter clothing, as if nothing had ever happened. Chris looked left and right, but the traffic and crowds had swallowed them all up – the woman, her two attendants, the bag thief . . . and Pavel Davidov.

Five

The connection at the other end picked up.

'Nicky?'

'Chris? Is that you?'

'I'm glad I caught you,' Chris began, desperate to tell Nicky the story of his adventure in Oxford Street. He cradled Aunt Helen's telephone more securely and sat on a tiny chair so that he could tell his story in comfort.

Before he could start, however, Nicky blurted out a question which left Chris hovering somewhere between standing and sitting, completely off balance.

'Have you heard the news?'

'What news?'

'About Pavel Davidov!'

Now Chris was very confused. Wasn't he the one supposed to be telling this story? He tried to readjust as Nicky poured out the news he had heard.

'He's gone missing! He didn't turn up for training yesterday, and when someone from the club went round to his house, the place was empty – and it looked as if it had been ransacked! United tried to keep it quiet, but the word crept out and –' Nicky paused. He could hear a strange, high-pitched noise on the line. 'Chris?'

At the London end of the line, Chris finally managed to bring himself under control. He hadn't realised that he had been almost screaming with amazement and excitement as Nicky spilled out the information. Now that there was a break in the flow, Chris jumped in quickly.

'I've seen him!'

'I know, I know,' Nicky sighed, thinking Chris had forgotten that they had both been at the Harvester restaurant.

'No, I mean today!' Chris yelled. He looked up to see his

aunt across the room, looking at him with a quizzical expression on her face. She was setting the table for tea in her small sitting room, putting out proper cups and saucers, plus fancy plates with flowery patterns, as if Chris was visiting royalty. Chris gave her a weak smile, which she returned on her way back out to the kitchen.

Meanwhile, it was Nicky's turn to react in amazement. It was easy for Chris to imagine Mrs Fiorentini with the same kind of disapproving look on her face as her son yelled into the phone.

'You're joking!!! Where? Are you sure it was him?'

Chris gave Nicky the edited highlights of events in Oxford Street, then had to go into more and more detail as Nicky spilled out a series of rapid questions. Aunt Helen passed back and forth, bringing in Fiorentini-style quantities of food, and signalling to Chris with her eyes that his 'quick call' was threatening to run up quite a bill.

Chris tried to speed things up, but Nicky kept latching on to certain facts and nagging away at them, such as when Chris mentioned the old woman and the reward. Nicky saw that as being very important.

'Will you give up about the money?' Chris insisted.

'No, but I mean, a pensioner giving you all that cash . . .'

Chris muttered something under his breath, then tried to explain again that just because the woman was getting on a bit, she didn't have to be down to her last couple of quid. Of course, he'd been under the same illusion himself for a while, but the woman had insisted that she could afford Chris's reward, especially since he had rescued a substantial amount of cash, not to mention all her credit cards and other valuables.

'Yeah, but thirty quid!' Nicky said, his voice showing how much he was in awe of Chris's fortune. 'Think what you could do with that!'

Chris had plenty of ideas of his own, and didn't need Nicky's help to fantasise about what £30 might be used for. He almost took the time to remind his partner that Nicky never needed much money of his own, since his family indulged just about every whim he ever expressed. At the last moment, he decided not to be uncharitable in the season of goodwill.

Instead, he demanded: 'Can we get back to the point? What should I do? Call the club? The police?'

'There won't be anyone at the ground, I bet,' Nicky replied, side-stepping the other possibility. 'We don't have a home game until the second week of January, and all the coaching staff and what have you must have broken up for the holiday.'

Only Nicky could have made Oldcester United sound like a bigger version of school. Chris smiled briefly at the thought of United's first team players, guys like Les Coventry or van Brost, running out of the gates, swinging their kit bags around and singing 'No more days of football, no more days of sorrow . . .'

'Someone must be there,' Chris said. 'If they really are worried about Davidov.'

'Dennis Lively was at home when the TV people spoke to him,' said Nicky. The story had been on the lunchtime local news.

'OK, what about Sean's home number?' asked Chris.

'Haven't you got it?' Nicky demanded in return.

'Yes, *at home*,' Chris replied with hard emphasis on the last two words to remind Nicky where he was. He heard a small clicking noise on the line which might have been his partner banging his head with the receiver.

'It wouldn't make much difference even if you did have his number,' Nicky reminded him. 'Sean was going away with his girlfriend over Christmas, remember?'

Chris opened his mouth, on the point of explaining the concept of the mobile phone to Nicky, but then said nothing. Seeing as he was in charge of the youth team squad, Sean Priest wasn't likely to be involved in the Davidov business. Plus, he might not appreciate getting a phone call from Chris while he was in some posh hotel in Scotland. Chris had never met this mysterious girlfriend of Sean's, but he had the feeling she would have heard all about the adventures Chris had dragged Priest into. No wonder they had gone away.

In fact, the odds were Sean would have turned his phone off even if he had stayed at home. He knew from experience how easy it was for Chris to get kidnapped or hired by the CIA. Chris figured maybe Sean was due a break.

'So . . .' Chris said out loud after a long pause. He was open to ideas. He was also starving, and the food on the table was drawing him closer.

'Didn't Pavel say anything to you?' Nicky asked. 'Anything at all?'

'No,' said Chris, although a memory was tugging at his sleeve, demanding attention.

'He didn't mention what he was doing in London? He didn't look surprised to bump into you?'

'He was definitely surprised to see me!' Chris laughed. 'But there wasn't really time to chat. I mean, one minute he was there and the next he'd gone.' He guessed what might be going through Nicky's mind at that point. 'At the time I didn't know he was missing, so it didn't occur to me to ask.'

'He's hiding, then,' Nicky said, with all the certainty in the world.

'Wait! I've got it!' cried Chris, almost choking on the first small bite of a cheese and pickle sandwich. 'Remember what Pavel said in the restaurant? His family arrive in England this week. I bet he came to meet them.'

'That could be it . . .' Nicky muttered in response, suggesting that he wasn't prepared to change his mind about Davidov's actions. 'But why would he be hiding? What about the burglary at his house? Why all the secrecy?' Those were good questions, Chris admitted privately. Nicky was still talking. 'Anyway, it means you can't call the police.' Chris tried hard to work his way through that last piece of logic. 'If he's done a bunk, that's up to him, isn't it?' Nicky explained. 'You can't get the police involved just because a bloke's showing his family round the bright lights of London.'

Chris struggled to keep up with Nicky's shifting train of thought. 'Yeah, but you said –'

Nicky jumped all over the unspoken objection. Chris knew his partner had a head of steam up now, and wouldn't be stopped until he'd got to whatever point he was aimed at.

'I mean, it's no business of the *police*, is it? And think of all the bad publicity there'd be if the *police* were seen sniffing around Pavel's private affairs.' Chris caught the emphasis Nicky had made. He knew full well where this was leading.

'So what are you saying, Nicky? That I shouldn't tell anyone that I've seen him? Despite the fact that the club are worried he's disappeared?'

He could almost imagine Nicky flicking back the sweep of jet black hair that fell across his forehead at moments like this, and the expression on his partner's face that meant, 'Well, not *exactly*'.

'Nicky . . .' Chris warned him.

'I just think it would be easier if we found out what was going on first. Then we could tell people . . . the right people.'

Chris was amazed at how neatly Nicky had steered the conversation so that although it was no business of the police what Pavel was up to, it would be fine for two teenagers to stick their noses in. For the moment, though, Chris had more pressing objections.

'*We*, Nicky?'

'Of course, partner!' laughed Nicky, as if he was offering to share the glory of a spectacular goal.

'Nicky, how are you going to find out anything up in Oldcester?'

'Never mind about that,' Nicky insisted, and then he added: 'Anyway, this is where the trail begins, up here at his house, right? Perhaps we could find out why he left . . . and meanwhile, you have all the other leads to follow . . .'

'Leads?' Chris cried. His aunt, who had just brought in a pot of tea (which seemed to signify that the afternoon snack she had promised was ready and that he should get off the phone), shook her head as she left the room, muttering about 'boys and their football'. It took Chris a moment to work out she must have thought he was talking about Leeds United . . .

'Nicky, it's Christmas Eve tomorrow! And I'm at my aunt's house!' He whispered the last part in case he was overheard. 'I can hardly go sneaking off, can I? What would I tell her?'

Nicky had no problem with that one. 'Last-minute Christmas shopping,' he suggested. 'After all, you've got that extra thirty quid.' Chris closed his eyes and imagined Nicky grinning at how easily he had anticipated that objection. He told Nicky he'd think about it, but he knew he was doomed to go along with the idea. 'Have you bought me anything yet?' Nicky asked, striking while the conversation was so completely under control.

'I have to go, Nicky.'

'OK,' Nicky said, sounding very pleased with himself. 'I have to go too. I'll speak with you tomorrow.'

Chris put the phone down and stared up at the ceiling. His

aunt returned with milk and sugar, and gestured for him to sit down at the table.

'Your father warned me about you two,' she said, which caused a moment of alarm before she added: 'Always on the phone to each other, even when you see each other every day.'

Chris smiled and nodded. And even when I don't see him, I end up doing what Nicky wants anyway, he thought. And after a moment's annoyance, that particular thought made him smile.

Six

By the following morning, Chris had more or less put the idea of going back to Oxford Street out of his mind. For one thing, it didn't make the slightest bit of sense. Just because he'd seen Pavel Davidov in the area once, it hardly meant he'd be there again. After all, how many of the thousands of people who had been milling around the shops actually lived or worked there? It was a place to go shopping. Davidov had only been in the country for a few weeks – maybe it made sense that he was just acting like a tourist.

Chris wondered if the woman he had seen was Pavel's wife. The more he thought about it, the more he thought they had been together, although there was a small doubt in the back of his mind. The Russian hadn't acted as if he knew her that well.

Chris was supposed to spend a quiet day with Aunt Helen, putting up Christmas decorations and fixing the tree. He couldn't imagine persuading her that he had to go out. His father must have told her that wherever Chris went, danger and trouble were always close by. Aunt Helen was on guard duty.

Besides, lying to his only auntie seemed indecent. There were some things Chris just couldn't do, not even for Nicky.

There was also the fact that having eaten one of his aunt's breakfasts, Chris could barely move. The first part of the morning drifted by dreamily, with a long read of her paper's sports pages (not that it took long – hadn't the *Daily Mail* heard of football?) and some chatter with her in the kitchen about what his father had been like as a kid.

It was while they washed up the breakfast dishes that Chris had his first proper look out of the window.

'What's that over there, Aunt Helen?'

Her eyes followed the direction in which he was pointing.

Off in the distance, half obscured in the dull wintry light, there was a grey smudge on the skyline.

'That's Canary Wharf,' Aunt Helen informed him. 'The biggest building in England. It's on the Isle of Dogs.'

There were a few tower blocks in Oldcester, but nothing to compare to the monster in the distance. Chris had heard of it, of course, but he had never imagined that a single building could stand out so clearly and from so far away.

'I couldn't imagine working somewhere like that,' Chris commented, shaking his head.

Aunt Helen laughed. 'You get used to being up high,' she told him. 'Where I work, I'm on the eighth floor, but you can't see much because of all the surrounding skyscrapers. We've actually got a better view from here.'

Chris looked out of the window again. As he pressed closer to the glass, he could see down to the street, five floors below. Cars sliced through the puddles left by hours of overnight rain, and the neon lights of the shops along the road were reflected up, bright and fierce in the gloom of an overcast day.

Opposite the block where Aunt Helen lived, there was some open parkland. It wasn't much. Just some patches of grass between cracked tar paths, and a sprinkling of bare trees. A set of black railings ran all round it, with roads like a black moat outside those. The flowerbeds were strewn with litter and the grass was thin and patchy. The small square was fine for walking the dog, perhaps, but nothing like Memorial Park, or the university campus near Chris's home, where he had played football for a year with a youth team called the Colts.

However, it allowed for a neat view from Aunt Helen's kitchen window, across the park to the close streets of terraced houses beyond. Looking off to the left, Chris could see the Post Office Tower, as grey as the clouds chasing behind it.

'What's this part of town called again, Aunt Helen?'

'Paddington,' his aunt replied, then she added, 'Like the bear,' as if that would help. 'The station is round the back from here.'

Chris nodded. After the adventure in Oxford Street, Aunt Helen had taken him to Piccadilly Circus, Trafalgar Square and a few other stops on the Monopoly board. Chris had the impression they had travelled in a wide circle.

'Are we far from Oxford Street – you know, from the shops?'

'Not really,' said Aunt Helen, and she gave directions, flicking soap suds from her fingers on to the window as she pointed. The road at the corner apparently led on to Edgware Road, and from there down to Marble Arch, and Oxford Street more or less continued from there.

'Did you need to go back?' Helen asked. 'I suppose I should have taken you to Hamley's. It's the best toy shop in the world, you know. I don't suppose you're too old for toys, are you? I'm never really sure what boys like you get up to these days.' She looked across at Chris with a worried look on her face, as if she'd bought Chris some Street Sharks figures or Subbuteo for Christmas.

'Not really,' said Chris, smiling, which seemed an adequate answer to both the questions she had asked.

'You couldn't get lost really,' Helen said, staring up at the slate-grey sky outside, 'but I don't suppose your father would approve if I let you wander the streets on your own. And I have such a lot to do if we're going to enjoy Christmas tomorrow!'

'It's all right, Aunt Helen, really. I'm not that keen to go out in those crowds again anyway.'

His aunt laughed and placed another plate on the draining board. 'You get used to it after a while. When I first came down here, I used to wonder how there could ever be so many people in one place! And I used to get lost all the time.'

Chris was on the point of telling her about San Francisco, which he had visited in the summer, and which had seemed pretty crowded as well sometimes. One good thing, though, was the way all the streets more or less ran in straight lines, which made it easy to find out where you were. Even Nicky would have found it hard to get lost in –

The phone rang.

Aunt Helen peeled off her Marigolds and went out to the tiny hall where the telephone lived. He heard her answer it, then put the handset down on the table. She bustled back into the kitchen looking just a tiny bit annoyed with the interruption.

'It's your friend Nicky again!' she announced, clearly quite amazed at how often two boys could talk on the phone. 'It's a terrible line; I could barely hear him.'

Chris gave her an embarrassed smile and went out into the hall, still holding the cloth he had been using to wipe up.

Aunt Helen was right. It was a terrible line. Nicky sounded as if he was calling from Alaska. There was an awful echoing in the background, and a dull, throbbing noise as if someone was revving up a bike in the phone booth.

'Nicky?' Chris began.

'Chris? Is that you?'

No, thought Chris, you've got the wrong number. Bad luck. However, Nicky was yelling so loudly at his end, Chris doubted that any subtle humour would get through to him.

'What are you calling for again, Nicky? Look, I've decided not to –'

'Can you come and meet me?'

Chris wasn't sure he'd heard right.

'What?'

'Come and meet me!!! I'm not sure how to get to where you are.'

Chris had a momentary vision of Nicky expecting him to go all the way back to Oldcester. Then Nicky made everything clearer. 'I'm at the station, Chris! In London!!!'

⚽

'You are stark raving mad,' Chris growled. He stopped, realising that he was talking to himself again.

'Have you seen this gear?' Nicky said, beaming. Yes, thought Chris, I saw it yesterday.

They were almost at the bottom of Tottenham Court Road. It had been an exhausting walk. The streets were every bit as packed as yesterday, plus everyone seemed to have an even more desperate air about them, brought on, no doubt, by the fact that they had less than eight or nine hours to find the perfect gift.

Nicky, on the other hand, was completely relaxed. 'Have you seen these digital cameras?' he sighed, spinning towards another shop window. Just like Aunt Helen, Nicky seemed to have the knack of diving through the crowds without making contact with anyone. Chris was bounced around like an NFL running back diving through the line of scrimmage.

'You take a picture, just like with an ordinary camera, only it's stored digitally. Then you download it to the computer and you can treat it just like a graphics file.'

'I know, Nicky . . .' Chris sighed.

'Just think what we could do with the web page!'

Chris had more important things on his mind than contributing to Oldcester United's internet home page. He tried to shut out the noise as Nicky babbled on. Fiorentini was very excited about the prospect of being able to take snapshots of the United stars and upload them into the web site. Somehow, Chris managed to break into the flow of his conversation.

'Nicky, would you mind explaining why you're here?' Chris asked for the third time. It had been a long walk from the station, but so far Nicky had evaded a direct answer as easily as he avoided the people on the crowded pavements.

'We talked about this last night!' Nicky snapped back, grumpily.

Chris tried hard to remember which part of the conversation had suggested it would be a good idea for Nicky to haul himself down to London.

'We're going to try and find Pavel, right? I could hardly do that up in Oldcester, could I? And it's not fair to leave you to do it all on your own.'

Chris mentally added 'Is it?' to the end of the sentence. Nicky had a habit of making everything into a question if there was any chance you might not agree with him. It was meant to imply that Chris had agreed to this thing once, so why were they going through it all again?

'You came all the way down from Oldcester this morning? Do your parents know you're here?'

Nicky made a face, suggesting that he was old enough to be allowed to fly off to New York if the mood took him, never mind just tripping down to London. All the same, Chris knew Nicky wouldn't be that stupid . . .

Nicky's explanation spilled out in a torrent, interrupted only a couple of times as someone pushed between the two boys. 'I didn't come down this morning, I came down last night. Well, not all the way here. I stayed at Paulo's in Hendon. Mind you, it took me almost as long to get here from his place as it would have from home! London's a big place, isn't it? Then I had to ditch Paulo this morning. He wanted to come with me, but I said I had to buy some last-minute Christmas presents for people, and I didn't want him seeing and blabbing to everyone. He's driving up to Oldcester tonight, so I have to be back at his place by six. That means I'm OK until about four, I guess. Would that be about right? Two hours should be enough to get back to Hendon. He'll wait anyway . . .'

They were at the corner of Tottenham Court Road and Oxford Street. Although it was still before ten, McDonald's was crowded. People spilled out on to the pavement with sesame seed buns crammed in their mouths. The entrances to the tube station were every bit as stuffed, with people slowly emerging into the dull daylight, hoping to find inspiration – or at least a cheap gift or two.

Chris pulled Nicky to a halt before they got caught up in the scrum.

'I meant why are you here at all, Nicky? What's this meant to achieve? We'll never find Davidov! Even if he was here again today, have you seen how many people there are?'

He indicated the crowds with a wide sweep of his hand. Nicky looked at them blankly, as if he hadn't noticed them before now.

'Aren't they here for the football?'

'What?' Chris almost choked on the question.

'I thought Spurs must be playing some kind of charity friendly or something . . .'

'What?!!'

'I knew it couldn't be a Premiership game or anything, because it wasn't in the papers, but . . .'

The penny finally dropped in Chris's mind. Tottenham Court Road. Spurs . . . Nicky thought they were near White Hart Lane! Chris was speechless. Nicky's ignorance of geography was pretty impressive, but Chris had never realised just how bad it could be.

'Never mind . . .' he sighed.

Nicky smiled brightly, his eyes sparkling. He flicked back the fringe of his hair, which he seemed to be wearing even longer these days, making him look more and more like a tanned, grinning Jarvis Cocker.

'Let's get on with it,' he said decisively. 'I don't have long. Oh, but one thing.'

Chris looked up, feeling almost as tired as he had last night when he had fallen asleep the moment his head hit the pillow of Aunt Helen's spare bed.

Nicky grinned again, a little more awkwardly. 'I'll have to find some presents while I'm down here. You know, for my cover story.'

Chris could hardly believe it. He was going to end up shopping all over again. Then an idea popped into his mind and he felt one small weight lifted.

'Follow me,' he sighed. 'I know just the shop you need, and it's right on the way . . .'

⚽

Nicky was delighted with his finds.

'These are so cool!' he laughed. Chris loitered by the till as Nicky queued to pay. It had taken his team mate a while to work out who should get the flashing Santa which played 'Jingle Bells', and to decide whether his aged grandmother would work out the mystery tune coming from the spinning-top snowflake. Chris suggested it might be 'Wonderwall'.

'She likes Oasis,' Nicky commented, lost in a dream world of flashing lights and squeaky tunes.

Chris looked away, which was when he realised the girl behind the till was looking at him oddly. She had a pale, skinny face, with wide, grey eyes. Her mouth drooped open in the rare moments when she wasn't speaking, which made her look pretty dumb. Chris pitied her. If Gillian Anderson worked in that shop for more than an hour, she'd end up looking as if her brains had been sucked out through her ears as well.

The girl was looking back at him. One of her incredibly narrow eyebrows shot up. 'I know you, don't I?' she asked abruptly, without pausing her rapid scanning of the barcode attached to a Santa's sleigh.

Chris heard Nicky giggle. 'I was here yesterday, with my aunt,' he explained, more for Nicky's benefit than for hers. 'Only I waited outside.'

'That's it!' the girl shouted, her voice a horribly nasal version of the dark-haired barmaid in *EastEnders*. 'You're the one who rescued that old dear's bag. Tripped up a mugger, didn't you! I saw you through the window.'

Several heads turned in his direction, attracted by the

klaxon-like quality of the girl's voice.

'Something like that . . .' mumbled Chris.

'You deserve a medal or summink,' the girl said, turning to repeat this to everyone in the crowded shop. 'That old lady nearly lost everyfink!'

There was a polite murmur of comment from the people in the queue. Chris could see Nicky in the middle of the line, grinning impishly. In that same moment, an idea must have popped into Fiorentini's mind, because he leant forward and placed the plastic Santa in Chris's hands.

'Good for you! Here, mate, take this as a reward,' he said, in his best mockney accent, stolen directly from *Thief Takers* (Nicky couldn't stand *EastEnders*). 'Maybe you've got a kid sister or a mate you could give it to. I think what you did was brilliant.'

Chris was speechless, and stood frozen on the spot, glaring at his friend. The other people in the queue looked at the small Father Christmas in his hands, and simultaneously six or seven reached into purses and wallets to dig out small amounts of money, everything from 50p to a fiver, dropping the cash into Chris's hands while he tried to find something more to say than, 'No, honestly, I mean, don't . . .'

Eventually, touched by Chris's heroism and Nicky's generosity, even the store manager chipped in with a novelty Xmas tree and a tenner in cash. No-one seemed to have noticed that Nicky's 'generosity' consisted of giving Chris an item he hadn't paid for yet.

Chris was dying of embarrassment. He was going to have a long word with Fiorentini when he got outside.

'Good for you, mate,' beamed the Tracy behind the till, restarting the business of topping up her boss's lost profits. 'That Mushy had it coming. Him and his mate.'

'Honestly,' said Chris, still reeling from the shock of it all. 'I didn't –' A coin dropped to the floor. By rights, it should have been a penny. 'Mushy?'

'That bloke you tripped up, the one that took the old dear's bag . . .' Tracy explained (fitting in a 'That'll be £22.14' somewhere in the middle).

'You know him?'

'Sort of,' she continued. 'He's a bit of a local character round here. He does a lot of work for the smaller traders – permits, contracts, that kind of thing. All the shop people know him. Plus, he has these other lads working pitches up and down the street. His mate Benny is just along the road; he sells dodgy bags and stuff; you know, counterfeit stuff that looks likes it's Gucci. Plus, this year, they've been selling stuff like we have in here; you know, novelty gear. Only it's nowhere near our quality, is it?'

That wasn't really a question aimed at him, but Chris felt compelled to answer: 'I've never seen stuff like you have before.'

The girl beamed widely and winked at her boss. 'Thanks!' she said. Chris had visions of his face being used in their advertising from now on – 'Boy Hero Says Our Santas Are Best!' Meanwhile, Tracy continued her tale. 'Mushy's supposed to be straight, you know, but a lot of the scam artists work for him. He did time, too, a while back, for shoplifting and dipping.'

'Disgraceful,' said the woman at the front of the queue. 'Vermin like that should be swept from the street.'

'That'll be £9.99,' said Tracy, who wasn't much interested in the woman's opinion, although she did make sure that one more piece of rubbish left Oxford Street, all nicely paid for and tucked in the lady's bag.

Nicky was next up. He was still grinning like a madman, so Chris had to look away. Once Nicky had been parted from twelve quid and was on his way to the door, Chris thanked Tracy and was about to leave when the manager appeared.

' 'Ere,' he said, in an accent that was even harder to cut through than Tracy or Nicky's. 'You like football, doncha?'

Chris looked down at his chest, where his Oldcester United shirt was showing under his open jacket. Chris had unfastened it the moment they came into the shop, which was like a sauna.

'Uh-huh . . .' said Chris, cautiously.

The guy gave him a leaflet; a badly printed piece of blue A5 paper. It had pictures of Teddy Sheringham and Gianlucca Vialli on the front. Or Julian Dicks and Mother Theresa, it was hard to be sure.

'Boxing Day morning, at Brentford's ground.' The manager pulled at his earlobe as if that might help him recall the rest of the details. 'It's a charity game. Oxford Street against Soho –

you know, the traders and shop managers and stuff.'

There was a £2.50 entrance charge, but the manager had written 'FREE' in big letters on the leaflet and signed it in a looping squiggle. 'Come along. Should be a lot of fun, and if you're there, it might make people dig a little deeper, you know? It's for the hospital.'

Chris started to explain that he was going to the Chelsea game that afternoon, but then decided not to mention it in case he was volunteered for any more fund-raising activities in the meantime.

'Will Vialli and Sheringham be there?' Chris asked.

The guy looked at him as if he had just asked about life on Mars and scratched at his ear even more furiously. 'Vialli's playing that afternoon, ain't he? For Chelsea. But what's Sheringham got to do with it?'

'Never mind,' said Chris. He thanked the manager and backed towards the door. Tracy yelled, 'See you Saturday!' and tried to start a round of applause. When this failed, she went back to her vacant stare and overcharged the next customer. Chris closed the door behind him as the argument started to build up.

Nicky was waiting on the pavement, clutching his flimsy bag to his chest and still grinning maniacally.

'How much did you get?'

'I can't believe you did that,' snarled Chris, turning away and stalking back up the street towards Tottenham Court Road.

'What?' Nicky laughed behind him. 'Hey, have you got my Santa?'

'Don't push it, Nicky!'

'No, but that's mine . . .' Nicky insisted, pulling up level with Chris. He looked around, realising that they were going back the way they had come. 'Where are we going?'

'We're going to see a man about buying even more of this rubbish,' said Chris, and there was a note in his voice that prevented Nicky from asking about his flashing Father Christmas for at least the next twenty metres.

Seven

'No refunds,' snapped Benny from behind the boards, without looking up. He continued to shift from one foot to the other, stamping his feet as if he was freezing to death.

'I don't want a refund,' said Chris, holding out the Santa. 'I didn't buy this here. I just want some batteries.'

'We don't do batteries,' he told Chris, managing an answer without appearing to pay any attention.

Chris sighed. The skinny man continued to dance, refusing to make eye contact. The fold-up tables in front of him, faced with black cloth, were filled with cheap versions of the tacky Xmas fare sold in the shop along the street, not to mention cheap watches, battered toys and keyrings. A small plastic tray contained a few Matchbox-sized plastic cars that spun crazily from side to side, tumbled, righted themselves and sped on. Almost the whole display was battery heaven, and everything squeaked, beeped, barked, honked, burped or talked merrily. No wonder the guy looked so miserable.

Not that the guy was going to admit that, of course. Reluctantly, Chris went straight to his one big bluff.

'Mushy said you could fix us up,' he said, with all the sincerity he could muster.

The man looked back at Chris, snapping his head to the front as if it were spring-loaded.

'When did you see Mushy?' he demanded

'Just now!' Nicky chipped in, which wasn't the way Chris would have continued. Still, he had little choice but to agree now.

'He was having a cup of tea in a caff,' Chris said, developing the tale. 'He saw what we'd bought, and said he knew where we could get fixed up with batteries. He told us to come and see you.'

'Berk,' snapped Benny, although just why he was so ticked off wasn't apparent right away. He looked dismissively at the Santa. 'Didn't that come with a battery?'

'It's worn down already,' Nicky replied. Benny shrugged as if it really wasn't his problem, and looked over their heads left and right, trying to catch the eye of someone who might be attracted to his pitch.

'Price of new batteries,' he said, without looking back at the boys, 'you might as well buy one of these.' He tilted his head back and bellowed 'Christmas novelties, ev'rythin' less than a poun'!' out into the street. No-one seemed that bothered.

Chris ignored the logic Benny was using, whereby a toy with a battery could cost less than a battery alone, and dug into his pocket for a pound coin. 'OK, let's do it that way.'

Benny reached for one of the motorised cars in the tray. Nicky moved quickly to put his hand in the way.

'Hang on, we want a new one!'

Benny shrugged. 'Suit yourself,' he said flatly. 'But with these ones at least you can tell the battery is working, whereas who knows with the ones in the packet, right?'

That idea had a strange kind of logic about it. Not enough to stop Nicky, though.

'That's no problem. We take a new one, open it up and if it doesn't work, then –'

'No refunds,' said Benny.

Chris picked up one of the cars and glared at Nicky to remind his partner that avoiding getting ripped off over a battery wasn't a priority. They hadn't exactly found out a lot so far.

'By the way,' he said, lowering his voice and leaning a little closer to Benny. The young man scratched at his thin, close-cut beard and leant forward too. 'Mushy was wondering if there's been any sign of the cops.'

'Cops?' asked Benny, jerking back and looking around furiously.

'You know, the filth,' said Nicky, assuming there had been a problem of translation.

Benny's eyes narrowed. 'I know you, don't I?' he asked suspiciously.

'No, but Mushy does,' said Nicky, straining their bluff to breaking point. They were gambling an awful lot on Benny not knowing everything Mushy was into. Chris knew how badly that plan would work if anyone ever tried it on them, but he was hoping that Benny and Mushy weren't that close.

'I dunno . . .' said Benny, slowly. 'You look more like one of the Soho mob than one of ours –'

Chris didn't like the way that sounded. 'Look,' he interrupted, 'we just work for Mushy up the other end of the street, OK? And all we're asking is if the cops have been round looking for him, after what happened yesterday.'

'What, that trouble yesterday? Why should the cops be looking for him? They never got involved, did they?'

There was no easy way to answer that, seeing as Chris had no idea what had happened after Davidov ordered him to leave. The news that the police had never been called was worrying. Fortunately, Benny continued to rattle off details without any further prompting.

'The big bloke didn't pay Mushy any attention after they took the bags off him. As far as I know, everyone got their stuff back, no-one called the cops, and Mushy did a runner.'

Chris shrugged. 'Look, he just got worried that maybe the big bloke called the police later, OK?'

Benny laughed. 'So what? He was long gone, weren't he? What's he so worried for?'

Chris tried to laugh back, but he was thinking so hard he found it hard to fake. 'You know Mushy!' he tried. He looked away from Benny's eyes, worried that he wasn't being very convincing. That was when he noticed a small suitcase on the floor at Benny's side, which contained about a dozen of the black leather handbags every woman in London seemed to be carrying. They were wrapped in clear plastic bags. One of them had a 'REKECT' sticker attached. Chris laughed. It was a bit much when even the reject labels were faulty.

'Yeah!' replied Benny, scratching at his beard again. 'Where's he been hiding himself anyway?'

'How should we know?' Nicky butted in, as helpful as always. Benny gave him another dark look.

'Was I talking to you? I thought you said you just come from seeing him?'

Chris dragged his attention away from the handbags and rejoined the conversation. He plucked inspiration out of the air. 'That was a while back. Over in the usual place.' He gestured off behind him, in a rough semi-circle that took in everything north of where they were. The opposite direction to Soho.

'The Eclipse? Bit early for that, innit?'

Chris gave him another 'Who knows with Mushy?' shrug. 'We'd better get back and tell him the coast is clear,' he said, taking a step back from Benny's pitch. Benny was looking increasingly suspicious, and Chris wanted to get out of the way before he managed to activate a few more brain cells and penetrate their 'disguise'. Benny's next words made him stop.

'You wanna remind Mushy that he's got a lot more to worry about than Lilly Law. He wants to keep his head down, if you ask me.'

I'd love to, thought Chris, but there was no way he could question Benny any further if he and Nicky were meant to be working the street. He pulled back a little further.

" 'Ere, you from Mushy's part of the world?' Benny said, taking a closer look at Chris for the first time. Chris felt himself losing control of the situation.

'Why do you ask?'

'You talk a bit like 'im, that's all. Plus you got one of them old Crystal Palace shirts, like he wears sometime.'

Chris saw Nicky bridle at the insult to their beloved red and blue, but he managed to jump in before his partner said anything he shouldn't.

'You think I sound like I'm from south London?' Chris asked.

'How would I know?' sneered Benny. 'I'm from Romford. Never been any further south than Upton Park.'

Chris drew a mental map in his head and decided that Benny's geography was only slightly better than Nicky's.

'We'd better get back,' he said.

Benny nodded, and looked away as if he was going to get back to 'work'. Then another thought fired off inside his mind. It was quite worrying the way it was warming up.

'Who's been watchin' your pitch, then?'

This time Chris couldn't beat Nicky to the ball.

'No-one! We sold out an hour ago. You want to see the money Chris has in his pocket . . . I'm telling you, our pitch is a hundred times better than this one . . .'

'What's the matter with you?' snapped Chris as they walked back up Oxford Street. 'What was the point of ticking him off like that?' Nicky was still smirking. 'It's like with that guy in The Wanderers the other day.'

'He had it coming,' said Nicky, without making it clear just which individual he meant. 'I hate people like that.' He did a very accurate impression of Benny's whining accent.

Chris found himself smiling briefly. Then he checked his watch, remembering just how little time they had.

'OK, now what?'

'We have to find this Equinox place,' Nicky replied.

'Eclipse,' Chris corrected him automatically, thinking while he walked. He was still on overdrive from the conversation with Benny. 'But where's that going to get us? What makes you think Mushy is going to know where Pavel is staying?' If he was staying in London, it was a very large place.

'I dunno,' said Nicky. 'It was your idea.'

Chris didn't remind Nicky that this whole crazy scheme was really his. Talking to Benny was Chris's one contribution, and only because he really hadn't thought of anything else at all.

'I bet it's a pub,' said Nicky. That made sense. Chris saw Nicky glance at his watch.

'It could be anywhere. We don't have time to waste looking for it.'

Nicky agreed. 'We need a phone,' he said.

Chris worked out quickly that Nicky was talking about looking up the pub in the phone book so that they would know what street it was on. 'It'd be quicker to ask someone.'

Nicky looked back at him blankly. 'No, I mean we need the phone,' he said, and he turned off the pavement into a small sandwich bar, having spotted a payphone sign in the window. Chris stopped, and was immediately shoulder-charged by a short man who looked a bit like Neil Ruddock.

Chris followed Nicky into the café, dodging any other tackles. By a miracle, the queue at the counter was tiny, so he bought them both some food and a can of drink. The miracle didn't extend to freeing up a table, so Chris walked to the back of the small shop, where Nicky was speaking loudly into the phone, covering his free ear to shut out the background noise.

All Chris could hear of the conversation was Nicky saying 'Yes' three times in a row, followed by 'Are you sure?' and a big grin. Nicky gave him the thumbs up as Chris put the food down on a small table, as if to confirm to Chris that the news was *that* good. Chris smiled back, then noticed that there was a phone book on a shelf under the table. He picked it up, but hadn't really remembered what he was looking for by the time Nicky hung up the phone.

'Thanks,' said Nicky, reaching for the food. Chris noticed that Nicky didn't offer to pay for it, but it could wait.

'What was that all about?' asked Chris. At the same time, he remembered he was looking for a pub called the Eclipse. He leafed the phone book open, but was quickly confused. The 'A's seemed to go on for ever, then the 'B's. He flicked to the back, and the book had only reached the 'D's.

Nicky was watching him, tucking into his food. Chris looked at the phone book again, wondering if they had a different alphabet in London.

'It comes in bits,' said Nicky, through a mouthful of food. 'You need the E to K.'

Chris worked out fairly quickly that Nicky didn't mean the book came to bits, and started looking for another directory. S-Z was next in the pile, then E-K. Each one of them was half the size again of the Oldcester phone book.

'London's a big place,' Nicky commented, which Chris thought was a bit rich given that Nicky had been moaning about how long it had taken to ride in from Hendon not an hour or so back.

'Eclipse, Eclipse,' muttered Chris.

'Look under F,' said Nicky abruptly, just as Chris was scanning the first few lines of the right page.

'What?'

'Look up Foster. Foster Associates.'

Chris looked up from the page. 'Who?'

Nicky repeated the name, although it was blurred by the large bite he took from his sandwich at the same time.

'Why?' asked Chris, aware that he was running through the usual list of one-word questions that Nicky demanded before he ever told his partner anything worthwhile.

'Because Laurie Foster is Pavel Davidov's agent.'

'He is?' asked Chris, impressed that Nicky had tracked this

down. 'How did you find that out? Who was that on the phone?'

If he was expecting the answer to be Dennis Lively (or anyone else connected with running the club), Chris was quickly taken aback by Nicky's answer.

'Russell.'

'Russell?' said Chris, a little loudly. He was getting tired of having to ask so many questions to get the truth out of Nicky.

Nicky wasn't paying attention. A man and woman sitting at a nearby table were pulling their shopping bags closer, as if they were about to leave. Nicky's eyes narrowed like a hunter spying prey, and he moved towards the table aggressively.

Chris mumbled under his breath, then slipped the phone book under one arm, picked up his food and headed for the table. It took barely a few seconds, but Nicky was already embroiled in an argument.

'Look, young man, I was next in line!'

'How do you work that out?' Nicky was shouting loudly. He flicked back his head and tried to stand up to the man, who Chris realised at once was several centimetres taller, a lot bigger and vaguely familiar.

'Look!' the man repeated, stepping closer to the table. 'I was at the front of the queue!' His voice was plummy and very posh. He spoke slowly, as if he was trying to remember each word separately and then get them out of his mouth one at a time. That was familiar too. Chris wondered why.

'Big deal!' sneered Nicky. 'We already got our food, so that puts us ahead of you.'

Chris took the last few steps towards the table. It was set against the wall, so that only one end was open. Two benches lay on either side, tight to the edges of the table. Nicky squeezed in along one, and was sitting with his back to the wall before anyone could interfere. The bench on the far side was empty.

Neither Nicky nor the man even looked at Chris walking up. In fact, neither did any of the customers, who were all turning to watch the free show. Chris found himself standing invisibly at the man's elbow, wondering just where he knew him from.

'You were using the phone!' the man insisted. The last word had the longest 'O' sound Chris had ever heard.

'And that disqualifies us from having a table?' Nicky retorted. The man gripped his gloved fists tightly, seething with rage. He had dropped what looked like a large black leather wallet on the table, but if he thought that was going to count as staking a claim, he didn't know Nicky very well.

The audience (almost everyone in the café, at that point) was enjoying the entertainment, and several of them nodded at Nicky's last point. The man, though, wasn't persuaded. He was very red-faced and his jaw tightened. A small vein throbbed on the side of his forehead, which Chris stared at as if he expected it to burst. He had been about to point out to the man that he could take the seat opposite, but that didn't seem to be an option any more. There was no way he and Nicky could continue to live on the same planet, never mind share a table.

The nagging feeling that he knew the bloke continued to tug at the back of Chris's mind. He looked about forty and he was tall with a receding hairline. He had a tired grey suit under a fawn floor-length raincoat. No bags, though, Chris noticed. He wasn't here for the shopping.

'Kids like you think you can get away with whatever you like, don't you?' the man spat angrily, which seemed to prove that he had given up hope of winning the argument by logic. 'Where I come from, we treat adults with more respect.'

Nicky shrugged. Fortunately, he didn't add fuel to the remark by suggesting that perhaps the man should go back home.

The man stiffened, stretching his neck as if he had cramp. Then he turned and faced Chris. A look of surprise went across his eyes, as if he was recognising somebody, then he spun round quickly and went for the door at speed. By the time he was out on the pavement, two people had started clapping (Nicky took a bow) and a pretty young woman with red hair had slipped into the vacant bench opposite Nicky.

'His loss,' she said, smiling at her good fortune. Nicky grinned back broadly, enjoying the glory.

Chris looked out on to the street for a moment after the man had disappeared. What had spooked him? It didn't make sense . . .

Still, whatever did make sense when Nicky was around? Chris put his food down on the table and settled on to the seat beside Nicky. It took him a moment to gain his partner's attention.

'You're in a very awkward mood this Christmas,' he said.

Nicky pushed his fringe back. 'Why do adults in this country think kids don't count in situations like this? We've got as much right to sit down as anyone, right?' He looked around, checking to see if anyone would cheer his statement, but everyone in the bar had turned back to their own meals now that the floor show was over. Even the pretty girl ignored him, burying her head in a magazine. 'It's not like this in Italy,' he added.

Chris knew Nicky had never been closer to Italy than a weekend school trip to Hastings. He tapped the phone book. 'Look up this Foster bloke, then,' he said, as he opened his can of Virgin cola.

Nicky made a small, disappointed face, put out that his moment of glory had been so short. He opened the book and flicked through the pages, back and forth, until he located the Fosters. After a moment of searching, he found the one they were looking for.

'Wardour Street,' he said. He looked up, as if he expected Chris to be able to explain where that was. Then his eyes opened wide. Chris watched as Nicky dived into his backpack.

'An A to Z,' said Nicky as he brought out his prize. 'Paulo lent it to me.'

Chris nodded, mentally cursing himself for not having asked Aunt Helen if she had one. He was reminded again how unprepared he was for this adventure. It still seemed completely unrealistic to be trying to find someone who was almost a complete stranger in a vast city neither of them really knew. Just like the phone book, the A-Z showed how completely different London was in scale to Oldcester. Their home town's Red Book was 24 pages of maps. The London A-Z was 108.

'Nicky, what did you tell your family?'

Nicky looked up. He had opened the book on a random page and scanned it quickly. His brow creased as he realised that he wasn't going to find their target that way.

'Didn't I say? I just told them I had to get some last-minute Christmas shopping, and that I knew this place in London where I could find what I was looking for.'

Chris found himself looking at the bag of presents tucked in the top of Nicky's backpack. He was sure they could have found similar junk in Oldcester, if they had just looked hard enough.

'Anyway, I had to get out of the house for a day or so. All those girls, taking over the bathroom for hours and playing dippy music on the stereo . . .'

Chris grinned. 'Aren't you worried that they'll just take over your room while your back is turned?' Nicky's face showed that he hadn't thought of that possibility before now. He pushed the phone book over to Chris.

'You better find this pub,' he said in a low growl, and then he found the index in the A-Z and started to track down Wardour Street.

Chris completed his task (and most of his early lunch) long before Nicky found the right page in the A-Z. Finally, though, Fiorentini stabbed his finger down on the page in triumph. 'Got it!' he grinned.

He sat back, holding the page open with his hand. The smile slowly faded as he realised there was something else he needed to know.

'Where are we?' he asked.

Chris leant forward to look at the page, with its crowded streets, twisting in every direction, the names changing almost every centimetre. Then he caught sight of a broad slash across the page just above where Nicky's finger was indicating.

'Look, Oxford Street!'

Nicky beamed brightly and stared at the page in a 'if you say so' kind of way. Slowly, he managed to put together that they couldn't be that far away.

The young woman on the opposite bench put down her magazine, looked at Nicky, Chris, the A-Z and her cappuccino and pointed back over her shoulder.

'That's Wardour Street over there,' she said.

The two boys looked past her, and out through the window at the front of the cafe. On the other side of the tightly packed street, there was the narrow entrance to one of the side roads.

'Brilliant!' said Nicky, who clearly thought this was a lucky sign. Moments later, Chris determined from the A-Z that they weren't far from the street where the Eclipse pub was either. 'Which first?' Nicky wanted to know.

Even though he was still convinced this was a wild goose chase, Chris was caught up in it enough now that he was thinking quite clearly.

'This agent guy first. It's Christmas Eve, Nicky. We'll be lucky if he's there at all, but I bet this Foster bloke will go home sooner rather than later. You know, to spend Christmas with his family.'

The sarcasm was wasted on Nicky. 'Good point,' he said, nodding quickly. He packed the book away, finished his food and drained the can. 'Come on, then,' he said. 'Let's get going.'

A middle-aged couple pounced on their seat before they were standing. Chris pushed Nicky through the door before he made any more new friends.

Eight

'And you are?' the receptionist asked. She didn't look up, but continued to stare into a small hand mirror while she plucked her eyebrows. Chris winced. Nicky was made of sterner stuff, though, and didn't look away. Chris guessed he must be getting used to the sight.

'In a hurry,' Fiorentini replied. 'Is Mr Foster in?'

Chris nudged his partner with an elbow. It seemed as if Nicky was having a real problem being polite to anyone this Christmas.

'No, actually,' the young woman replied, completely ignoring the tone in Nicky's voice (maybe she had a younger brother, Chris decided). Her eyes opened wide while she checked the effect of her work with the tweezers, as if she was auditioning for the role of Frightened Woman in a horror movie.

The phone rang. The receptionist was wearing a headset, so all she had to do was reach out a finger (complete with garish pink fingernail), press a button on the telephone and she could perform her duties without looking away from the mirror. At first, her phone voice was as phony as the one she had used when Chris and Nicky arrived at Foster's office. Then she started talking like Barbara Windsor.

'Sandy!' she squealed into the mouthpiece. 'Are you nearly ready? Yeah? Yeah!!! I know!!!' Chris couldn't hear the voice on the other end of the line – the most he picked up was a faint squeak from the headset, as if it had mice inside. Sandy's information was obviously very amusing, though, since the girl broke into a large fit of the giggles, a sound like water gurgling down a narrow pipe. The squeaking mice were drowned completely.

She looked up and realised her visitors were still there.

'Hang on, Sandy. I know!!! I know!!!! Look, he's not here, all right? I don't know if he'll be back, but I'm locking up the office in five minutes. It is Christmas Eve, you know! Half past, Sandy, right? I know!!! Don't!!!'

Chris finally realised she had been talking to them in the middle of that burst of speech, and not just to Sandy. It was hard to tell. She hadn't covered the small microphone or changed the tone of her voice at all.

'Do you have any idea where Mr Foster is?' asked Chris, as politely as he could manage. There was a door behind the girl's desk, which presumably led to an inner office. Chris wondered if she was covering for him.

The girl flashed him a filthy look in the middle of a long string of 'Yeah!'s and 'I know!'s.

'He went out for coffee half an hour ago, and he's meeting someone for lunch at one. That's it! That's all I know. I know!!! Sandy, that's wicked!'

Chris was ready to give up. The receptionist was starting to throw her make-up equipment into a huge leather bag. Chris knew that she was going to be out of here in a lot less than five minutes and didn't want to get caught in her way.

Nicky, though, wanted one last try.

'Do you know Pavel Davidov?' he said loudly. Apparently even Sandy heard that one because the small squeaking noise disappeared. The receptionist paused, holding her bag open on her lap. It was one of Benny's Rekects, Chris noticed, and the handles looked ready to break.

'Who?'

'Pavel Davidov.'

'Who are they?' the girl demanded. Then she added, 'I dunno. A couple of kids,' which must have been for Sandy's benefit.

Nicky tried to make himself taller, clearly offended by that description. All the same, he continued with considerable patience. 'It's not a they, it's a who. A footballer. Laurie Foster is his agent, right?'

'How should I know?' the receptionist cried angrily. It seemed a difficult question to answer quickly.

'Mr Foster does have footballers on his books, right?'

The girl shrugged. Clearly, her knowledge of Mr Foster's business only went as far as knowing which drawer of the desk contained the paperclips.

Even Nicky decided to admit defeat this time, and the boys turned to leave the office. As they did so, Chris noticed one of the blue fliers pinned to the noticeboard, advertising the charity game. He pointed it out to Nicky.

'He'll be there,' the girl called from behind.

Chris hesitated a moment before turning round, since the odds were she was talking to Sandy again. When he glanced back over his shoulder, he saw that the girl had swept the headset from her head, untangling it from a vast pile of permed blonde hair. She looked directly at him while she plucked her coat from a hook on the wall at her side. The bag hung from her shoulder.

'The game?'

'He organised it,' she said hurriedly, now on her way towards them. The two boys found themselves bundled out on to the landing. 'He does it every year. The record company people play the traders from Oxford Street. Laurie knows all of them, and he organises the game and everything. He gets all the best players to turn out too.' She turned to lock the unmarked wooden door.

'Like who?' Chris asked, but he guessed before the girl even opened her mouth that she would have no idea. Nor could she explain what these 'best players' had to do with either the record companies or the Oxford Street traders.

Her keys rattled as she turned one in the lock. She gave Chris a brief smile and clattered down the steep stairs on her high heels, vanishing out of sight before either Chris or Nicky could think of another question. They were left standing on the landing, quite bemused.

'What an airhead,' muttered Nicky.

Chris was almost prepared to agree. He looked at the closed door as if it had just slammed in their faces.

'No name,' he said, a moment later.

'What?'

'No name,' Chris repeated. 'On the door. And did you look around in there? If he really represented any famous players, don't you think the waiting room would have pictures?' There had been photos of a few pop acts Chris had never heard of – big-haired girl singers and ageing boy bands.

Nicky could see where Chris was headed now. 'You think he's a fake?'

'Could be,' Chris replied. 'In any case, it all seems a bit cheap and tatty, doesn't it? I can't imagine this guy does any real business with Premiership players.'

Nicky agreed. They stood there for a moment longer, considering what they knew. Chris could sense that Nicky was itching to write some facts on paper.

There was a shriek from downstairs, plus a clattering noise. Chris looked down the stairwell.

'Come on,' Nicky said, 'let's get out of here.'

They started towards the stairs. The office was up on the third floor of a tiny building in the middle of Wardour Street. Chris hadn't looked closely at the nameplates of any of the other offices, but he had the strong impression there weren't too many multi-national companies in here. He remembered Benny talking about the south side of Oxford Street as if it were bandit country.

Just as that thought popped into his mind, Chris heard someone talking on the stairs. There were heavy footsteps on the floor below, coming closer. Chris was behind Nicky, so it took him a moment to reach the next turn in the stairway and see who it was. He knew at once, by pure instinct, it was trouble.

The heavy footsteps were being made by just one man, although there were two coming towards the team mates. Chris recognised him at once – big, very ugly, with hands the size and shape of house bricks and thick eyebrows that met in the middle of his heavy brow. All his clothes looked as if they had been washed at too high a temperature.

It was no surprise to see the Bajoran behind his hulking mate. The second guy looked up, and caught sight of Chris just as Chris saw him. His pale skin looked yellow in the dull light of the stairwell, save for a dark purple mark on his cheek, the size of a 50p coin. Chris wondered what had caused that. Looking down from above, Chris could also see that the guy had a bald spot in the middle of his head that was more like £2.50 in loose change.

Behind these two, the girl from Foster's office was on the floor, picking up fallen lipsticks, eyeliners and other secretarial equipment. It seemed the strap on her bag had broken. She looked up, and her eyes showed a great deal of anxiety when she saw Chris.

An alarm bell went off in Chris's head, loud and shrill. He had no idea why. They were just two guys who had been in the street at the time of the incident with Pavel and Mushy. Sure, they looked like the kind of heavies who routinely turned up in *NYPD Blue*, but Chris had no logical reason to be worried.

Which was why Nicky was a bit slow in reacting when Chris yelled 'Run!!!'

⚽

Chris moved in from the left, the ball at his feet. He could see Nicky on the other wing, slightly ahead of him. The defenders were playing flat across the back, and it was easy to play a chip just beyond the last guy, putting Nicky clear behind them.

'This'll be number four,' Nicky laughed.

Chris smiled broadly too, as he angled his run into the box. His marker came in tight, but Chris was goal side, and had smuggled himself between the defender and the ball. Racing in off the wing, Nicky had a free choice – shoot or cross.

Schmeichel stayed back on his line – probably nervous of being chipped again. As Neville came across to try and make the tackle, Nicky unleashed a powerful shot aimed at the near post.

Schmeichel's save brought a gasp from the capacity crowd and a loud cry of amazement from Motty. Nicky threw his hands up in dismay. But the rebound fell kindly for Oldcester, and Chris only had to move a fraction of a centimetre to put his head behind the ball and guide it safely into the net.

The crowd were silenced. All John Motson could find to say was: 'That's his hat-trick!' Chris and Nicky joined the rest of the team duck-walking near the halfway line . . .

'That's a stupid way to celebrate a goal,' Nicky said, and he and Chris leant closer together to bang heads and high five.

The gorilla watched them, his thick eyebrows almost knotted together as he frowned. He threw his controller on to the desktop.

'You two are cheating,' he sulked.

Nicky's face was a picture of wounded innocence. 'What? How could we have cheated? You were watching the screen! All we did was change the names of a couple of Oldcester's players!'

Chris tried to keep a straight face. Nicky was almost telling the truth. They hadn't cheated at all while Tank had been watching; they had just edited the names so that they could be part of the Oldcester line-up. However, Nicky had dropped his controller, and he and Tank had got into a right tangle trying to retrieve it from under the desk. That gave Chris more than enough time to type a few quick commands into the computer, making sure that their namesakes had stats good enough to beat Brazil at home, never mind Manchester United in a friendly at Star Park.

Tank refused to play for the last three minutes. Oldcester ran in three more goals, allowing Nicky to claim a hat-trick as well as Chris. The last goal was a free kick by Piet van Brost, curled in from 35 yards.

'That would never happen in real life,' snarled Tank.

Chris had memories of a game when Man U had stuffed five past Oldcester, the year United had gone down. Chris smiled at the memory – not long before, he had met Peter Schmeichel up at Old Trafford. They had got on really well, and when Manchester had come down to Star Park later in the season to hand out the 5–0 thrashing, Schmeichel had dropped off two Manchester first-team shirts, one each for Chris and Nicky. They had been signed in marker by both of the teams, and Schmeichel had added a PS: '5–0. Ho, ho!'

One of Chris's favourite daydreams was to imagine playing for Oldcester up at Old Trafford, and reversing the scoreline against Peter and the rest of the Reds. OK, some of their players might be getting on a bit by then, but that didn't matter in the dream. What counted was that Chris wanted to have revenge.

Walloping United 7–1 on Fifa '98 wasn't quite the same thing, but it would have to do.

Snake put down the phone.

'I can't find him,' he said, curling his lip in distaste as he looked at the two boys celebrating. 'He must have his mobile turned off.'

Chris waited to see what this meant. He and Nicky were seated in front of the computer, on one side of the more spacious office that lay beyond the receptionist's cubicle. Tank had wandered off to the side, into one of the darkened corners, where he stood with his arms folded and his huge turret of a head drawn into his shoulders.

Snake had been pacing backwards and forwards across the carpet while he made call after call. They had been here at least 30 minutes; probably longer.

'So, what happens now?' Nicky demanded.

That seemed a fair question, although it was clearly too difficult for Snake. Even though he counted as the brains of the outfit while he was with Tank, he wasn't much of a thinker.

Between them, the two men had captured Chris and Nicky easily. Running hadn't been that good a plan in the first place, but it was made worse by two factors. One, there was nowhere to run to. Two, Nicky's reactions on being told to flee for his life from a threat he knew nothing about had been to turn round and say 'What?' He had watched Chris's back disappear round the turn in the stairs, and stood there open-mouthed as Snake and Tank came up alongside him. They had marched him up the stairs back to Foster's office, where Chris had been waiting for them, having realised Nicky must have been caught.

The girl hadn't gone up with them. Chris couldn't make up his mind if that was a good thing or not.

Snake had obtained her keys. He opened the plain door and let them in. After a few questions he had decided to seek guidance from his employer. Meanwhile, Chris and Nicky had discovered the Fifa '98 box and a couple of joypads, and talked Tank into playing a game while Snake ran up his boss's phone bill.

The game was over now. Snake rubbed the top of his head with his knuckles as if he was trying to wake up the brain cells one by one. The big earring jingled.

'I'm going to ask you one more time,' he snarled. 'What was you doing here?'

Snake was trying hard to be threatening, but he was cursed with one of those high-pitched voices like Alan Ball's, which made it hard to sound really tough. He could jab his finger and clench his fist as much as he liked, but it was still like being given the third degree by the cute blue thing off *Sesame Street*.

'We came to speak to Mr Foster,' Chris said in a tired voice.

They had explained all this already.

'But he ain't here!' said Snake, who had a knack for stating the obvious.

'That's what his secretary said,' Chris agreed.

'Yeah, right!' Snake cried, as if Chris had just admitted something really damning. 'And Gloria left! So what were you doing here then?'

'We were leaving too,' snapped Nicky, whose voice sounded a lot more dangerous. 'Remember, you caught us on the stairs.'

'Yeah! Caught you!' whined Snake, who wasn't catching on too well. Chris decided to try and put him out of his misery.

'Look, we came here because we heard Mr Foster was Pavel Davidov's agent. You heard of him?' Just in case there was any confusion, he added: 'The footballer?'

'Yeah, yeah, I know,' Snake insisted, although Chris doubted that he was much of a football fan. 'What makes you think Mr Foster's got anything to do with this Paffel bloke? And what's it to do with you, anyway? What makes you kids think you can break in here?'

'We weren't breaking in!' Chris shouted back. 'Do we look stupid enough to go round breaking into places? We came to see Mr Foster because –'

He paused for a moment, remembering that there was part of the story he didn't know. He turned to his partner, who was engaged in a staring match with Snake.

'How did we find out that Foster was Pavel's agent?'

'Russell broke into his house,' said Nicky, between gritted teeth.

Snake's attempt at a cruel smile grew wider. Chris sighed.

'What?'

'It wasn't nothing serious!' Chris noted how Nicky's voice was sliding more and more into his fake London 'wide boy' accent, and how he was adopting Snake's sloppy talk. Nicky loved all that 'sorted' nonsense. 'We thought it would be worth a look round, to see if there was anything left that would give us a lead. You know, summat to say where Davidov might have gone. Russ found this letter, and –'

'Are you out of your mind?' Chris yelled, completely ignoring Snake, who was trying to interrupt. 'You and Russell can't just decide to break into people's houses!'

'Why not? He wasn't nicking anything. Besides, someone

must have been there before, because there was a broken window at the back and the place was in a mess, just like it said on the news.'

This was interesting news, but Chris still felt unhappy at the way they had come by it. 'So, Russell didn't actually have to *break* in . . .?' he asked.

'Well, sort of,' Nicky admitted. 'The cops had boarded up the broken window, so Russell had to pull that off. Does that count? He made sure he put it back again . . .'

Chris threw his head back and glared at the ceiling, rocking back on the chair. He and Nicky were alike in so many ways, but there were times . . .

'Anyway,' Nicky said, continuing the explanation, 'when he got in, all he found was this letter from Laurie Foster, explaining how he was going to be Pavel's agent, and that he was taking over all his financial affairs.'

Chris heard the words, but he didn't react to them, at least not directly. He allowed the chair to fall back to the floor and stood up. The action brought him right in front of Snake.

'OK, I was wrong. Apparently we are that stupid. But we didn't come here to break into Mr Foster's office, we came here to ask if he knew where Davidov had disappeared to.'

'On Christmas Eve?' asked Snake, who was still determined not to believe anything he heard, although he didn't look so sure now that Chris had marched up in front of him.

'I know. That's stupid as well. He's not here. We shouldn't be either. So now we're going.'

Chris brushed past Snake so quickly, the balding man didn't have time to react. There were plenty of full backs who had had the same problem in the past. Chris went through into the receptionist's area, then stopped and turned round. Snake had turned to look at him. He had his hand on Nicky's shoulder, preventing Fiorentini from following Chris any further.

'Aren't you forgetting something?' Snake sneered.

'Oh, give up!' Chris snapped back. 'What do you think this is, a TV show? I'm leaving, and you're letting Nicky go so that he can leave too.'

He turned away at once and went to the outer door, pulling it open. He heard a small squeak from behind him, which he assumed was Nicky wondering if Chris was abandoning him. However, Snake apparently let Fiorentini go at that point, because he caught Chris up on the landing.

'Nice bluff!' Nicky chuckled quietly. 'Now let's get out of here!'

He flew down the stairs ahead of Chris, taking them two at a time. Chris followed at a more measured pace and reached the building's front door some time after Nicky, who was bouncing up and down on the pavement anxiously.

'What are you waiting for? Come on, before they change their minds.'

Nicky was about to turn back towards Oxford Street when a hand fixed on the sleeve of his coat. He was yanked back, and looked past his shoulder, expecting to see Snake and Tank. But it was Chris. And he didn't look as good tempered as the two toughs.

'I want a word with you,' Chris said, in a low, fierce voice.

'What?' Nicky cried defensively.

'This just ended, Nicky. Enough is enough. You're going home and I'm going back to Aunt Helen's.'

Nicky was gobsmacked. 'What for? We're just starting to get somewhere.' He glanced at his watch and showed it to Chris. 'Look, it's not even one o'clock yet; we've got plenty of ti–'

Chris wasn't having any of it. 'I'm going with you to the station, and you're getting on a train back to Hendon. Then I'll go back to Aunt Helen's. Hopefully, she won't ask where I've been all morning, so I won't have to tell her any more lies.'

Nicky still didn't get it. Chris cut off his protests with a cutting swipe of his hand. 'I'm not arguing, Nicky! I'm telling you. This is none of our business and it doesn't make sense. It's Christmas Eve, and in a few hours my dad is going to arrive at Aunt Helen's flat, and he's going to ask what I've been doing for the last couple of days. He isn't going to be impressed if he finds out that you and I have been running around Soho chased by a couple of rejects from *The Bill*.'

Nicky started to make some kind of protest, but Chris wasn't in the mood to listen. He still had a few complaints of his own left.

'How could you ask Russell to break into Pavel's house?' Chris yelled, loud enough for people around them to look in their direction. Chris glared at a few of the spectators, then dropped his voice a little anyway. 'We don't have any right to do that!'

'But he's in some kind of trouble,' Nicky replied quickly. 'We're just trying to help.'

'How do we know he's in trouble?' Chris fired back. 'Because his house is in a mess? Maybe his cleaner took the week off. Because he sloped off down to London? He could be Christmas shopping!'

'What about Snake and Tank and that Foster guy –'

'What about them? So Pavel's found himself a dodgy agent. OK, it's a mistake, and maybe we could do something – maybe we could talk to him after the holiday. But we shouldn't be breaking into his house and running round London after . . . after . . .' Chris dried up. He couldn't even remember what they were supposed to be looking for.

Nicky didn't say anything for a while. He and Chris walked slowly back up Wardour Street, towards the crowds flooding back and forth along Oxford Street. It wasn't the first time they had argued like this. Over the last few years, Chris and Nicky had found themselves being drawn into all manner of adventures and escapades. They didn't go looking for trouble, but they seemed to have an unerring instinct for finding it.

Very often, there came a time when Chris lost confidence like this. Nicky knew that Chris was usually the one who came up with all the really good ideas for getting stuff worked out. His job was to make sure they kept going. Right now, Nicky believed if he could just sit Chris down with a list of all the things they had discovered, he could persuade him to –

He shook his head. Chris had a determined look on his face that showed he wasn't going to listen to any arguments. Nicky rehearsed a few in his head just in case, but said nothing.

They crossed Oxford Street and found a turning on the other side, which started off just as packed, but slowly thinned out a little. There were restaurants and coffee bars on both sides, and Nicky could hear people laughing and having a good time. He started to feel quite depressed. Perhaps it wasn't right to be away from home on Christmas Eve. Perhaps he was missing his family after all – his dad, his mum, his sisters, his baby brother, his gran . . .

Uncle Fabian, his cousins . . .

Julianna, Paulo's girlfriend and now Alex-flipping-andra . . .

'Look, Chris,' he began.

'Who were you talking to on the phone in the cafe? Was it Russell?'

Nicky nodded. Chris was still marching northward along the street, aiming them in the general direction of the railway station. There was a thoughtful look in his eye. They were slowing down, too, although that might have been because they were approaching a crossroads.

'And he told you about the letter, right?' Nicky nodded again. 'What else did he say?'

'There wasn't much else,' Nicky confided. 'Russ didn't find anything else in the house. He just made a few suggestions.'

Chris was biting his lip. They pulled up at the kerb.

'Like what?'

'Oh, I don't know. Places we could try looking for Davidov. The Russian Embassy. Any Russian clubs or stuff. He said we could look in the phone book and –'

Nicky looked left and right, seeing that the road was clear. Chris's gaze was fixed almost directly ahead. They stood there in complete silence for another ten seconds at least.

'This isn't our business,' Chris muttered at the end of the pause. Nicky wasn't at all sure if his partner was talking to him or not. 'And it's pointless,' Chris continued. 'We have maybe another couple of hours at most before you have to get back on the train.' Nicky didn't answer that either. 'Plus,' Chris began, and then he swung round to face his team mate. 'You have got to stop picking stupid arguments with people. What was that all about in the cafe?'

'Is that what's been niggling at you?' asked Nicky, sounding almost relieved.

That was part of it. Chris knew that the argument had put doubts into his mind, but he just hadn't been able to figure out why. But standing on the pavement, on a street he didn't know the name of, in the middle of a huge city he barely understood, it all suddenly jumped into place.

'The same bloke!' he cried out.

This was a little too obscure for Nicky. 'What?'

'It was the same bloke! The guy in the cafe . . . and the guy at The Wanderers!' Chris lifted his face to the sky and almost shouted it out again, relieved at last that he had made the connection. 'The same guy!!'

'Are you sure?' said Nicky, who hadn't recognised the man at all.

'Positive,' said Chris. 'We couldn't see his hair and face the other day, because of that dumb hat and scarf. But I remember his eyes, and that wallet-book thing he was carrying. And you must have heard his voice that first time – didn't you recognise that odd accent?'

Nicky screwed up his face, trying to recall the two occasions. None of what Chris was saying jogged his memory at all.

'So, what are you saying? You think we're being followed?'

Nicky's voice betrayed his nervous excitement. Chris felt the same buzz too, but for different reasons.

'I'm not saying that,' said Chris, but he didn't offer any alternative.

'So . . . there is something to this, after all?' said Nicky, the corners of his mouth lifting.

Chris nodded. Nicky's smile broadened.

'Great! Because look – on the corner. It's that pub – the Eclipse!'

'I know,' said Chris, not bothering to look. Once again he had turned to face the opposite corner. 'I saw it as we came up the road. The only problem is that we aren't going to be allowed inside, are we?'

'We could just say we were looking for someone.'

'Not the sneakiest way to slip in, is it?' Chris pointed out.

'So how else are we going to find Mushy? Wait for him to come out?'

'Maybe we don't need him,' said Chris, and he was grinning confidently as he pointed towards a smart, white-painted building on the opposite corner, which had a restaurant on the ground floor.

'The Odessa?' asked Nicky, reading the sign. 'So?'

'Look harder, Nicky,' said Chris quietly. 'It's a Russian restaurant.'

Nine

The menu on the outside of the restaurant was written half in Russian, half in English. The English half wasn't much easier to understand.

'What's "bliny"?' asked Nicky, screwing up his face just at the sound of it.

'Who knows?' Chris replied. And at £24.99, who cared? 'We don't have to eat anything, Nicky; just wait inside and maybe ask a few questions. Look, it must be the only place along here which isn't chock-full. There's even a table by the window. We can say we're waiting to meet someone, have a coffee and some kind of cake or something, and keep an eye on the Eclipse while we're in there.'

Nicky wasn't happy. Eating in anything other than an Italian restaurant was almost a betrayal of his heritage. Plus, he could see that an awful lot of the dishes on the menu featured cabbage, turnips or some other suspicious-sounding vegetable. Not a hint of pasta. They worked out that bliny was a kind of pancake which came smothered in soured cream.

'Remember I have a train to catch,' he whined.

They moved towards the door. As they were about to push it open, Chris pointed out the tacky blue poster above the sign showing what credit cards were accepted. 'Looks like this is the big event round here over the holiday,' he whispered. Nicky ignored the cheap poster and continued to look miserable.

The Odessa's manager appeared a little fed up with life as well. When he saw that his new customers were just a couple of kids, one of whom was a scruffy individual with hair like a bird's nest and the other who looked as if he was on his way to a dentist's appointment, his welcoming smile vanished. He tried to argue with them about taking the window seat, but

Chris insisted that 'Daddy' would be arriving shortly, and they wanted to keep an eye out for him.

They ordered some cans of drink (£1.50 a pop!) and some overpriced pastries and sat in silence for a few minutes, watching the street outside. The restaurant was deathly quiet, as if the few customers inside realised they had made a terrible mistake. The staff were pretty sullen and lifeless, except when two of them started arguing. The fight was in Russian (Chris guessed), which made it harder to follow, but Chris got the idea that it started off being about how clean the cutlery was, and then moved on.

Nicky normally loved a good fight, but he was still keeping watch out of the window. He didn't even touch his cake, which was another sign he wasn't enjoying himself.

Chris turned back to face the main room of the restaurant. It was a large room, divided by screens made from cane, draped with climbing plants. It was a long way from the kind of place he and Nicky normally ate in.

Just then, Chris heard the word "futbol' shouted loudly by one of the two arguing waiters at the end of a long sentence of loud words. Two customers were rising to their feet nearby, pulling on their coats and picking up hats, gloves and belongings in a hurry. The shouter snapped on a creepy smile and went over to help the woman with her bags. Behind his back, the other guy made a gesture with his hand which was probably not all that polite. Then he caught sight of Chris looking and wandered over with his pad open and his pen poised.

Chris was in no mood to add to the bill, so he wasn't sure what to say for a moment. He offered the waiter a sheepish grin.

'You into football?' he asked. He noticed a small badge on the guy's lapel and added 'Yuri', just to be friendly.

Yuri, a tall, young bloke with black hair, a thin moustache and eyes like flies trapped in amber, stood over them with pen poised, clearly trying to work out what part of the menu sounded like 'Yuinto.' Chris tried again, using the tactic Brits always use when faced by someone who can't speak English.

'Do . . . you . . . like . . . football?' he said loudly and slowly.

Yuri got the message this time. 'Football! Yes!!' He jabbed himself in the chest a few times with the biro. 'Spartak

Moskva!' He reached out with his pen-holding hand and flicked Chris's jacket open a little wider. 'Bayern Munich!' he grinned.

'No . . .' said Chris, as he realised Yuri's mistake.

'Crystal Palace!' Yuri tried again, smiling broadly. It came out as 'Creestul Platz,' but Chris got the idea. He jumped in before Yuri went through any more teams who had stolen United's red and blue strip.

'Oldcester United,' he explained. Yuri's smile twitched and faded a little. Chris groped for another idea.

'Here . . .' muttered Nicky, and he dived into his backpack, which was lying on the floor at his side. His search led to half the table being covered with Nicky's essential survival equipment (including the A-Z, a diary, some folded greaseproof paper – Nicky had probably eaten a packed lunch on the train – a thick pad of lined A4 paper, a compass(!), a *Rothmans Yearbook*, a junior *X-Files* novel and a packet of tissues). However, in the end he found what he was looking for – the programme from the last Oldcester United home game.

'South-ham-peton,' Yuri read slowly.

'No . . .' explained Nicky, with a tired sigh. 'We were the home team, Oldcester United.' He opened the programme and pointed to a shot which had the whole squad in first-team strip, with the Virgin logo displayed across the broad stripes. Chris hoped fervently Yuri didn't read that out loud.

'I have not heard of this team in Russia,' the waiter said apologetically. 'Over here, I am watching Chelsea.'

Nicky's eyes brightened and he started to explain that Chelsea would be facing United at the Bridge on Boxing Day, but he stumbled when he decided Yuri might not know when Boxing Day was.

In the meantime, Chris had been struck by a moment's inspiration.

'Yuri, look . . .' he said, grabbing the programme. He turned to the right page at once, having looked at it several times on the day of the Southampton match and several times since. There was a match report and several colour photos from the game before, away at Aston Villa. United had won 1–0 thanks to a van Brost penalty in the first half. For the next 60 minutes they had been pinned back by attack after attack, every one of which had been broken up by the solid tackling of United's defence. And one man in particular had played out of his skin.

Chris jabbed his finger down on the photo he had recalled. 'Pavel Davidov!' he announced. 'He used to play for –'

'Dinamo!' cried Yuri with great pleasure. 'Yes, I know him!'

He called over the other waiter, who had just collected his tip from the table vacated by the fast-moving man and his wife. This guy had a tight, surly expression on his face until he saw the picture. There was Dwight Yorke climbing high off the ground, looking to reach a high cross. Behind and above him, a giant in red and blue had his forehead firmly behind the ball. His face was distorted with the effort of making the challenge, but it was instantly recognisable.

The two waiters spoke to each other in an excited babble of words, some of which were almost recognisable. Yuri turned to the programme's cover and tortured the word Oldcester. His mate said it had to be Manchester, and then they started arguing again.

Somewhere in the middle of the row, three things happened at once. First, Yuri started pointing excitedly at one of the neighbouring tables, and then out into the street, in the vague direction of the houses opposite. His mate frowned.

Second, their loud exchange of opinions attracted the attention of the manager, a short guy with a heavy gut, dark receding hair and a sharp black suit. He walked over briskly, calling something in a stage whisper, at which the two waiters started speaking even louder.

And the third thing . . .

'Chris!' hissed Nicky. 'Look!'

Something was nagging at the back of Chris's mind, insisting that he didn't want to miss the conversation between the Odessa's staff, even if he didn't understand a word of it. The manager seemed to be trying to shut Yuri up, but the waiter was having none of it. All the same, Nicky's voice sounded urgent.

Chris looked round quickly. His team mate was pointing out of the window. Chris turned in his seat and looked across the road. On the corner opposite, there was a dark figure in a grimy black coat, who had just emerged from the Eclipse. He scratched at his beard, then opened his mouth as if he was talking to someone still hidden in the doorway.

'Mushy,' sighed Chris.

Their target looked as unwashed, unkempt and unsavoury as Chris remembered. Nicky had managed to pick him out from the description alone. As soon as Chris confirmed they had acquired their target, Nicky started to pull his belongings back towards his bag.

'Come on,' he hissed. 'We don't want to lose him!'

'Hang on,' Chris whispered in reply, holding up his hand to halt Nicky. Fiorentini looked up. He was completely surprised to find Chris had turned his back on the window and was paying attention to a rumbling conversation in Russian.

'But you said Mushy was our only lead!' Nicky squealed.

'Just a minute!' Chris demanded.

It was true that yesterday he had believed that if anyone knew where Davidov had gone after the confrontation in Oxford Street, it was the street rat. It was a pretty slim chance, but Nicky had agreed that someone like Mushy might wonder why the man who had robbed him of the stolen handbag hadn't handed him in to the police. Plus, even then, Chris had thought there was more going on than just an accidental encounter between a bag snatcher and two metres of Russian footballer.

But Chris's instincts were going haywire now. His understanding of Russian might have been non-existent, but some words hardly change no matter what language they are spoken in. Like 'futbol'. And people's names.

There was a lot of shouting and hushing and pointing and looking round going on between the three men, none of which made sense. But one thing was clear. They were still talking about Davidov, and it didn't seem likely that they were discussing how well he had marked Yorke out of the Villa game.

'Chris!'

Ignoring Nicky's pleading voice, Chris tried to break into the argument the Russians were having. It didn't work. The three of them had formed a tight circle, and each was shouting into the faces of the other two from a range of five centimetres.

'Chris, look!'

This time Nicky's demand was so urgent Chris had to look round. Mushy had moved away from the pub door a little, leaning back on a smart silver Saab. Three other 'gentlemen' had come out of the doorway and were glaring at him hotly.

Mushy didn't seem that bothered by their hostility. He was shrugging and gesturing with his hands.

The three men stood in a wide semi-circle. Two of them were very familiar people already. Snake was at the near end of the line, trying to look hard and menacing. Tank was at the far end, blocking most of the pavement.

Between the two stood a tall man in a smart sheepskin coat, the kind only football managers and sports commentators wear. He was wearing dark glasses, even though the day remained dull and overcast, and he was smoking a large cigar, from which rich blue smoke curled up before it was snatched away by the wind.

Foster.

It was immediately clear that Mushy and the other three weren't playing on the same team. Tank and Snake seemed very keen to get to grips with the hustler, but Chris had seen the same thing they had. Mushy had a set of keys in his hand, which he was dangling alongside the door of the gleaming Swedish car. Before they could damage him, he was saying, he would have done a lot of damage to something that cost a great deal more to fix up.

Foster gave the other two some kind of order, and they both relaxed. Snake made that curious shrugging, neck-stretching gesture all villains make when they are trying to look tasty. He signalled to Tank, and the two heavies vanished back into the Eclipse.

There were a few more words spoken between Mushy and Foster, and then the street rat turned away. After watching him for a moment, Foster crossed the street and headed towards the restaurant.

'He's leaving!' hissed Nicky, his eyes fixed on Mushy.

'Follow him,' snapped Chris, the decision being made quickly and instinctively.

'What???' demanded Nicky, several steps behind. 'What about you?'

'I'm going to take Foster,' whispered Chris with a nod of his head, indicating the tall, polished man in the long brown coat. 'Stick with Mushy for as long as you can. We'll either meet up here, or if you have to catch your train, you can leave a message for me at Helen's.'

Nicky was all ready to argue, but Mushy was moving

quickly, heading back towards Oxford Street.

'Go!' Chris insisted.

Even though he wasn't comfortable with the idea, Nicky grabbed his bag and headed for the door. Chris stood as well, intending to retrieve the programme before he set off after Foster. Part of him also wanted to hear the end of the Russian argument.

He heard the bell above the front door jingle merrily and looked round to give Nicky the thumbs up as he left. Only it wasn't Nicky going out. It was Foster coming in.

Ten

Chris sat down again, very quickly. He watched as Foster entered the Odessa, looking around over the heads of the few customers. He didn't seem to notice Nicky, who stepped aside to let him pass, made a cross-eyed face at Chris and scooted through the open door.

Foster's arrival was also noted by the manager, who made a strangled noise in his throat, pushed aside the surly blond waiter, and strode over to Foster. He held his hand out, indicating the back of the restaurant. Foster took one look in Chris's direction, or perhaps it was just at the table, and then he followed the manager to a table behind the cane screens. Chris avoided eye contact by the simple device of staring out through the window, where he could see Nicky in the street, trotting off in pursuit of Mushy.

Yuri and his mate were still scowling at each other, but the blond one heard the manager snap his fingers and scuttled off. Chris looked round as Yuri dropped the programme on the table. The waiter then made a very thorough job of scraping some non-existent crumbs from the tablecloth.

'What was that all about, Yuri?'

'Pavel Davidov,' Yuri whispered. 'Great player; big trouble.'

Chris leant forward, hoping to hear more. He tipped some cake crumbs off his plate for Yuri to sweep.

'What kind of trouble?'

'Russian trouble,' said Yuri, tapping the side of his nose and winking. As far as Chris could remember, that gesture was supposed to imply 'you know what I mean . . .' Perhaps it meant something different in Russia.

Fortunately, after a long look over his shoulder to make sure no-one was paying him any attention, Yuri added: 'Money.'

Chris nodded as if he understood, though he wanted to hear more. Just then, though, almost magically, the manager reappeared behind Yuri and barked an order in Russian which had Yuri buzzing away towards the kitchens at top speed.

Chris remembered there was an option to do Russian in the sixth form. He'd have to consider that, when the time came.

The manager stood by the table, puffed out his chest so that it at least equalled his belly, and drew himself up to his full height, which wasn't that full.

'Your father has not come yet?' It was phrased as a question, but the knowing twist of his lip showed Chris that the manager wasn't buying that story any more.

'No, not yet,' Chris replied quietly.

The manager found a single crumb that Yuri had left behind, tutted and picked it up on his fingertip.

'But your . . . brother, he leave . . .'

'He has a train to catch,' Chris said, a little more boldly.

The manager nodded, as if that sorted everything out. He looked down at the table and stretched out his pudgy, darkly tanned fingers to turn the programme so that it faced him.

'Old-ces-ter,' he said, in slow, accented English, one syllable at a time. 'Playing well this season, yes?'

Chris nodded, then watched as the manager flicked idly through the pages. 'Very good at the back. Very solid. Of course, they make a good transfer, yes? A big Russian defender.' He pronounced 'big' just as Pavel Davidov would have – 'beeg' – as if there was all the time in the world to get the word said. 'Many players come here now from the old Union. Kinkladze at Manchester City; Kanchelskis at Everton.

'Not all of them fit in so well,' he said, and he finally reached the page that showed Yorke and Davidov challenging for the ball. There was a moment of silence. 'Sometimes, they come to my restaurant for a taste of the old country, you understand?'

Chris nodded.

Apparently, that wasn't the end of the lesson. 'In Russia, before perestroika, I was college teacher. I teach Western languages; French, German. Good job. We make many fine students. But then come Gorbachev, Yeltsin –' He almost spat out the last word; Chris knew at once that he was not a fan. 'Russia cannot pay for anyone to teach Russian. How can they pay me to teach French?' He sighed deeply.

'So, I come to West. I think maybe Germany or France, where I speak the language good, and can get good job. But it was not to be. I must borrow money to bring my family out of Russia. The people I borrow money from say I must come to England, where I do not speak so good. And I must manage restaurant.'

Again, he spoke the word as if it hurt his mouth to have it inside. Chris wondered what all this was about. The manager was looking out of the window still, but not at the street any more. Chris could see that the older man's dark eyes were gazing all the way back to the Kremlin . . . or wherever he called home.

Those same eyes then flickered down at Chris. 'Mafia,' he said.

Chris felt a little tug of apprehension at the word. His father was a big fan of old movies, and Chris had been brought up on a steady diet of *The Untouchables* and *Godfather* films. He knew what the word meant.

Only . . .

What did a bunch of Sicilians or Yanks have to do with Russian teachers running restaurants?

Chris filed the question in the back of his mind to get sorted out later. The manager was already speaking again.

'Many more like me,' he said, tapping the programme. 'People who have problems. But this is a Russian thing . . .' He leant forward, lowering his voice to a whisper. 'It is not something for outsiders to get involved in.'

Chris kept silent. Warnings about keeping out of things were his speciality.

'I have heard there is young boy looking to find someone. He ask many questions. Other people are looking for this same person, and they hear the questions the young boy ask, and they wonder if he will lead them to what they look for. Perhaps . . . it would be best if the boy did not look at all.'

Chris let the words run around his head. Not a warning, then. Advice. Sensible advice, from someone who knew Pavel's story. Perhaps he had been told it over dinner one night.

The manager leant back, perhaps seeing in Chris's eyes that

the rouble had dropped. He put on his jolly welcoming smile. 'I think your father meant a different restaurant for you to wait at, yes?'

Chris smiled back. 'I think you're right.' He stood up, pulling back his seat. The manager smiled even more brightly. 'Could I just use the toilet before I leave?'

'Of course!'

The manager waved theatrically towards the back of the restaurant, and Chris went past him, walking quickly past the cane screens. At the last moment, the manager realised where Chris was going, and there was a worried squeak, but Chris had no intention of making any more trouble. He just wanted a closer look (and a leak wasn't that bad an idea . . .).

Foster was sitting at a small side table, operating a calculator, his forearms framing a steaming plate of soup. Chris gave him a hard stare. Foster was still wearing the dark glasses, and the sheepskin coat had only been slipped from his arms – he had it draped around his shoulders and the back of the chair. Chris decided the agent's hair was dyed, and noted the heavy jewellery on his hands and wrists.

Then he walked past.

There was only one other table occupied at the back of the restaurant, or at least that was how Chris read it. The diner was actually absent, but there was food set out and an open briefcase on the tablecloth. Chris glimpsed inside as he walked past. What he saw made his heart miss a beat.

The manager was still at the front of the Odessa when Chris returned, tucking his shirt into his jeans and walking briskly. Chris was handed his few belongings, including Nicky's programme. Yuri tried to hand him the bill, but the manager shook his head briskly. From what Chris saw of the total, it was just as well.

The manager held the door open and wished Chris a cheery goodbye, as if he was a valued and regular customer. Chris skipped down the two steps and on to the pavement, turning quickly away from the door and along Mortimer Street. Not before he reached Tottenham Court Road, which was as crowded with people as before, did Chris look back over his shoulder. And only when he was sure that he wasn't being followed did he draw a deep breath.

He reached under his shirt and pulled out the leather

wallet. He was on the point of looking inside, when a voice yelled behind him. It turned out to be nothing to do with him, but Chris decided some more distance was in order. Zipping the wallet back up, Chris tucked it inside his jacket and crossed the road at a brisk trot, his heart hammering and his mind playing through the gory bits of *Godfather I*, *II* and *III* in painful detail.

⚽

His first thought was to go straight back to Aunt Helen's.

Perhaps the images playing in his mind were too strong, but he dismissed that idea in case hard-faced gunmen crashed in and killed everyone in her building.

His second idea was to find somewhere quiet and private where he could inspect his find. Rationally, Chris knew he wasn't frightened of Mafia hoods or anything like them (well, not *very* frightened, not all the time), but he knew that what he had just done was very wrong.

Chris wished Nicky was here to listen, or to share some of the blame. At the same time, after the going over Chris had given him concerning Russell and the break-in, he didn't want to get Nicky involved.

What had possessed him to do it? What if it wasn't *the* black book?

Chris's mind continued to race as he paced the streets of west London, looking for a refuge. From the moment he had seen the smart leather case with its faded gold lettering, he knew exactly who it belonged to. Well, not exactly; he couldn't put a name to it but he knew the face clearly.

Chris had almost felt like stretching for the case right then, when he first saw it. But caution had stayed his hand. He had no idea where the owner might be, and he didn't want to be caught.

He had found the loo behind a series of doors, along a dark passageway. His visit there was very brief. Someone was in one of the stalls, and Chris couldn't think who else it could be other than the man from The Wanderers and the café, the man who he was now sure was following him. It would have been nice to be sure, but Chris had doubted that it would help his plan if he banged on the door and asked to get a closer look at who was inside.

Instead, he had rinsed his hands in a hurry and rushed back to the restaurant. Emerging into the dimly lit rear room, all he had really been able to focus on was the open briefcase and the black leather case. What did it contain? A notebook? A set of lockpicks and a car jemmy? A gun? Chris cautioned himself to be sensible. He had flicked his eyes around the room; Foster had his back to him and was engrossed in a ledger and the calculations he was making. All the restaurant staff were out of sight.

And so . . .

Almost without thinking, Chris had walked briskly by the table, slipped his hand into the briefcase, and he had the wallet tucked in the back of his jeans before he met the Odessa's manager and Yuri at the front of the restaurant.

He had been gripped by a chilling fear of discovery even then, and it had not dulled now. The afternoon was darkening all around, which Chris knew made it more and more unlikely that he would be seen, but he couldn't shake off the feeling that every person on the crowded streets was watching him.

For one thing, it all seemed so unreal. Surely it didn't make sense that the guy would have just left the case unguarded. Maybe he thought no-one would be *stupid* enough to take it. Well, he hadn't reckoned with Chris, then . . .

All the same, Chris felt that he'd been set up. The more he thought about it, the more he was sure that the case had been turned towards the wall when he went back through the restaurant, but had been facing towards him as he went back. He ran the episode through his mind again, in slow-motion replay with a little white circle highlighting the case, and Alan Hansen remarking that it was very sloppy defending.

The bright lights of a bookshop beckoned. It was a big store, on a corner flanked by wide pavements, and with a small park in the square opposite, making it look almost separate from the huge, bustling city all around. Chris jogged across the road.

There were plenty of people in the shop, hunting for last-minute presents, but very few of them were in the history section. The shop was warm and filled with nooks and crannies, including some small seats under the windows on the first floor. Chris found one unoccupied, in a space from where he could only be seen from a very small part of the store, and slipped the leather pouch out from his jacket once more.

He tugged on the zip with trembling hands. The wallet was expensively made, well padded and had a metal fastener. It slid back with a soft buzz, and Chris opened the wallet on his lap.

What he discovered made his heart beat a little faster. It was a hi-tech electronic organiser, an even better version of the model Chris had been staring at in the shop windows of Tottenham Court Road. Slightly smaller than a paperback book, it had a smart keyboard, a small LED screen and special keys to access the diary, planner, address book and all the other functions. The casing was brushed metal, smart and silver. It was a little worn with use, but still perfect. An adaptor lead and serial interface cable were tucked into a compartment on one side of the wallet.

Chris managed to prevent himself drooling over the machine itself, and thumbed the on-key. There was a soft, high whine, like a hard drive spinning into life, and the screen came alight, glowing brightly in the low light of the window seat.

Chris licked his lips, wondering where to start. The address book seemed the best place, or maybe the diary. What Chris wanted most of all was proof that he had nicked the organiser from someone connected to Davidov, and not someone who had been unlucky enough to need the loo in the Odessa just as Chris walked by . . .

The diary. Chris keyed it open, and the page opened on today's date. He was hoping that it would have an entry like 'International Criminal Association lunch meeting, 12pm', something that would confirm Chris's suspicions about the owner – whatever those suspicions were. And for all he knew, maybe that was what he did find – there was a note of the Odessa's address, and a time – 2pm. No name, though. The guy was alone, after all, Chris remembered.

He keyed back a couple of days. This time, he saw something that made a little more sense. The entry read 'DL, OUFC, 9am'. It might not have made a lot of sense to most people, but to Chris the initials jumped out at him easily. OUFC – Oldcester United. That made DL Dennis Lively, the club's chairman, a larger-than-life figure who had kept the small city club up there with the big boys, not with stacks of money like a Jack Walker, but by sheer strength of will and sound judgment.

It didn't exactly put the organiser's owner in the international criminal mastermind class, but it did prove one thing. This had to be the guy Chris had seen twice before, in Oldcester and London, the guy Nicky seemed to attract like a magnet. Maybe he wasn't following them, or maybe he was, but one way or the other he was caught up in the same game they were playing. If he was looking for Davidov, the club was the smart place to start. Chris wondered if there was any way he could find out just who had been to see the United chairman.

Chris flicked over to the address book for a moment, to check something else. Sure enough, Pavel Davidov's address in Oldcester was there – a house the club had found him and his family when he arrived. The same place Russell had sneaked into.

Sadly, there was no other note against Pavel's name, and nothing under Secret London Hiding Places. Chris went to the Fs, to see if Foster was there, and he was, with the Wardour Street address and one other, out in Surrey somewhere. Chris bit his lip. At least this tied things together.

The one thing it didn't do, of course, was explain who the organiser's owner was. Chris wondered if there might be something at the beginning of the addresses. He started to scroll forward, but stopped immediately.

Another F had caught his attention.

Chris stared at the entry for several minutes, then started a search through the Ss. He found what he expected.

He and Nicky were both in the organiser. Names, addresses, phone numbers. Even Chris's internet address. Whoever had been snooping around after Davidov had found a connection to them.

This had just stopped being funny.

Chris was on the point of shutting the organiser down, when something made him search through the Notebook function, to see if there was any mention of himself, Nicky or Davidov in there. And there was. The writer had made extensive notes, notes which undoubtedly explained everything that was going on. On the most recent page, Chris saw his own name three times.

The only thing that stopped him wrapping up the whole thing right there and then was that he couldn't read much of anything except for the names of some people, the Odessa, and words like London and Oldcester.

Because the whole thing was written in Russian.

Eleven

Chris walked out of the bookshop, his mind in a turmoil. His rash decision to pinch the wallet had ended up making things even more complicated. Not only was it the wrong thing to have done, but now it was clear the owner would easily work out who had pinched the machine, and could track Chris down.

Visions of hard-faced gunmen with old-fashioned machine guns flickered into Chris's mind again. He thought about deleting his name and details, but decided it wouldn't make a lot of difference.

The man with the strange accent had been in Oldcester, pursuing connections to Davidov. He had somehow connected him to Chris and Nicky – perhaps because of the Harvester incident. If he was prepared to chase down leads like that, he must want Pavel really badly. But why? And just how far was he prepared to go to find him?

He tried to clear his head of the nagging fear that this adventure was spiralling out of control. It wasn't likely that he was in any great immediate danger. There was no way the organiser's owner could know about Aunt Helen's place – was there? She wasn't in the diary; Chris had checked. This meant the guy would have to go up to Oldcester, find out they weren't at home, quiz the neighbours until they found someone – like Dr Loenikov, several doors down, who knew where they had gone – then come back and . . .

Chris muttered under his breath. OK, it could be done. But not right away. He had a few hours to think, surely. In that time he could call Nicky, who would be back home, and tell him what he had found out. Of course, that also meant trying to persuade Nicky he had to move his whole family out of the house on Christmas Day in case they were gunned down by the Mafia . . .

'Perhaps Nicky could just speak to some uncle or cousin or something, and get us off the hook,' Chris joked to himself, nervously. Nicky always liked to joke about his family's 'connections' back in Italy. Sadly, they were completely made up. It might work on some of the morons from Blackmoor school, but Nicky's 'family' wasn't going to frighten this guy.

OK, back to the real world. The best Chris could hope to do for now was put Nicky in the picture. Then what?

Why was it so hard to make sense of all this? Chris felt as if his mind was stuffed with cotton wool. He felt like running the length of Oxford Street, yelling at the top of his voice, just to blow the cobwebs away.

That need had drawn him out of the close, cozy confines of the bookshop and back on to the street. He crossed the road and walked along beside the small park. It was a tiny area, just like the one outside Aunt Helen's building, fenced off by railings and a couple of gates, ringed by tall, bare trees swaying slowly in the cold wind. The flowerbeds were equally lifeless, with just a few shrubs and bushes to lighten the cold earth.

There was a patch of grass in the middle though, about the size of the two penalty areas at Oldcester, laid side by side. There were 'Keep Off The Grass' signs at intervals around the edge, and a sign just inside the gate had a large list of prohibited fun, including skateboarding, cycling and every imaginable ball game.

Chris grinned. The kids playing football there obviously didn't read too well.

⚽

It was impossible to find space on such a small surface. They were eight a side – nine on the team Chris had talked his way into. Almost every blade of grass had someone on it. In addition, the ball was a cheap plastic affair. It bounced wildly each time it hit the ground and swung crazily in the wind.

These difficulties made close control and fast reactions even more important. A player's first touch on the ball had to be perfect, otherwise he would be pounced on by defenders from all sides.

A wild pass upfield made Chris stretch his legs as he chased it. One of the other team's defenders was close up behind him. Chris slowed to let him get even closer, then trapped the ball on his left foot, dragging it back between his own legs and the defender's. He span round to his right at the same time, rolling off the other guy's body, using the defender to help keep his balance. It was too cold for the other guy to move quickly enough to foul him . . .

Chris had that vital half-metre of space. Other opposition players reacted at once, turning to face him. Chris looked up, and knew he had just one chance to make a decent pass.

There was only one other really decent player on his team, a long-limbed lad with dark, curly hair. He was so tightly marked, there wasn't room to pass him a piece of paper, never mind the ball. Most of the other guys on Chris's team were smaller than their opponents, which was probably why they had been losing 12–2 when he arrived. He had no idea how they had picked the teams, but the aim hadn't been to have a balanced game.

One of the smaller lads was loitering near the far post, in just a little patch of open space. The avenue between them was narrow, but Chris struck the ball fiercely, directly at the lad's legs. The kid's eyes widened as he saw the ball racing towards him, and he swung his right foot in a desperate attempt to volley it home.

He missed completely, but it didn't matter. The ball cannoned off his left knee instead, and flew just inside the post.

The first the kid knew of 'his' goal was when his team mates hoisted him off the ground. Their shouts echoed around in the cold air, clouds of vapour rising from their mouths. Their opponents looked around darkly, wondering who to blame. For some reason, at 13–8, they felt cheated.

Chris ran back to the middle of the pitch with his 'team'. They were having a great time putting one over on the opposition. Toby, the lad who could play a bit, jogged over slowly and gave Chris a one-handed slap across the palm.

'Nice goal,' he said. 'Ben's furious.'

He nodded towards the oldest boy on the other team. Chris had already worked out that this was the guy who had organised the game and picked the two teams. Ben was at least seventeen and much bigger than all of the others, but he was heavy, slow-footed and even slower at thinking. His face had a sulky, hard-done-by expression as he collected the ball from a flowerbed and complained to his team mates about how they were making mistakes.

'Doesn't lose often, then?' Chris said, smiling very slightly.

Toby, who was about the same age as Chris, smiled even more broadly. 'No, you're right there. Ben and his mates play together all the time. The rest of us don't get together that often – I've missed loads of games. Basically, though, anyone who isn't one of Ben's mob gets to play against him and his mates, and they normally thrash us.'

'They're still five goals ahead now,' Chris reminded him, putting a bit of space between them as Ben prepared to take the kick-off.

'Yeah!' called Toby. 'Where were you half an hour ago?'

Chris didn't reply, and he didn't think about what the answer could have been. Instead, he focused on the game. The standard of play might not have been very high, but the cramped pitch and the fact that most of his team were a year or two younger than their counterparts made it hard work. Even in the cold December air, Chris had shed his jacket and rolled up the sleeves of his shirt. The ground was slick underfoot, and he had been down a couple of times making challenges.

The playground at Spirebrook wasn't much bigger than this patch of grass, but even there Chris had always played a passing game, relying on the skills of Nicky and Jazz to find space and then make use of it. Here, although Chris could still make telling passes himself, he could never be sure what would happen to the ball afterwards. That forced him to do a lot more of the work himself.

Chris was strong on both sides, but he wasn't as gifted with the ball at his feet as Nicky and he knew it. His strengths lay in his fierce shot, his power in the air and the gift he had for ghosting into the box, slipping markers and finding room to score. Training at Oldcester had improved his dribbling skills, but there was nothing like a frantic game like this to make him realise he needed to work even harder on this side of his game.

He used his team mates where he could, even if it was only a faked pass to send a defender the wrong way. They wouldn't have minded all that much if he had kept the ball to himself all the time. They were enjoying having revenge on the older lads. During another break in play (13–9), a wiry, fast-running boy named David told him how the last couple of times they had been beaten by twenty-plus goals. Chris's team mates were a rough and ready collection of whoever else happened to be around. Toby only came to London when his father wasn't away on business – Chris got the impression the family were wealthy and had some huge place in the country. David's mum was a reporter, and left him with his married sister when she went abroad. The goalkeeper barely spoke English and there was another lad who didn't know the rules of the game . . .

'It makes it worse that we don't know each other,' said Toby as they waited for yet another kick-off (13–10). 'I wander over here on the off-chance there's a game, but you never know who'll be around.'

In some ways Chris was surprised there were so many guys prepared to turn up on the off-chance. He had never realised that so many people actually called the city their home. These kids actually lived in the middle of all the frantic bustle of the shopping streets and the tall office buildings.

'You're the best player we've ever had on our side!' giggled Mickey, a lad of about ten who ran like a greyhound – and played football like one.

'Yeah!' said David. 'Are you going to be living round here?'

'I'm afraid not,' said Chris. 'This is just a visit.' He saw a few of the faces around him fall slightly. 'Let's make the most of it, right?'

They picked themselves up again. Ben and one of his mates tried to mark Chris out of the game. There was nothing nasty about it, but Chris knew they had had enough of watching the ball fly past their keeper. The two of them bumped him a little and tried to keep him away from the action.

Chris saw Dave pick up the ball on halfway, and set off on a diagonal run away from him, moving wide, hand high. As he called for the pass, Ben and two others were all over him.

Dave took the chance Chris had opened up, ran directly on goal and fired in a shot. The keeper parried the first attempt, but Mickey poached the rebound. The three players around Chris looked at each other, realising they had been suckered.

'Thirteen-eleven!!!' Mickey chuckled as he ran back. Chris slapped him on the back.

'Nice goal,' he said, as genuinely as he could. 'The keeper wasn't expecting you to knock it in with your backside.'

Mickey laughed louder than ever, almost dancing back to their half. Chris pulled his fingers back through the wild tangle of his hair, breathing hard. He took a look around the park.

It was dark now, and the street lights outside the small square didn't throw a lot of light inside, especially round the edges and under the trees. But Chris saw there was someone watching the game. He didn't really recognise who it was at first, but there was something . . .

The game restarted, and Chris had to snap his mind back to the football as one of Ben's mates tried to dribble right up the middle. Chris dispossessed him with a neat touch, managed a one-two with Dave, then took off along the wing, closely shadowed by Ben. Chris shielded the ball with his body, faking turns this way and that as he looked for room.

He looked up once, and realised what it was about the lone spectator that was attracting his attention. The man's face was in shadow, but the bright glare of the nearest street lamp was catching the bottom corner of his coat. A long, brown affair . . . sheepskin.

Chris stumbled over the ball and gave away the throw-in.

Foster. Chris cursed his ill luck. How had the agent tracked him here? Or had he just been walking past, heard the lads shouting and come over to take a look?

Chris ran back towards the goal, where his dark baseball jacket was helping to mark one of the posts.

'What is it?' called Dave.

Chris said nothing until he reached the goal. Dave met him there, looking worried.

'I have to go,' said Chris. 'I had no idea of the time.'

Dave looked crestfallen. At 13–11 they were so close . . .

'Sorry.'

'I understand . . .' Dave sighed. 'Will you be around again?'

'I doubt it,' Chris said in a low voice. He looked over to the edge of the square, but now the bright patch of light was empty. 'Damn . . .' he muttered.

Dave's lip was twisted in disappointment. 'Yeah,' he said, as if agreeing with Chris. 'If you and the lad who was here yesterday could play for us a few more times, we'd thrash them.'

Chris nodded, trying to feign interest, while he searched

rapidly through the pile of coats. He found his jacket and slid his hand into the pocket, feeling the leather case tucked inside.

'Good was he?' he asked. He looked up to see if he could see any sign of Foster, but there was none. Dave was also looking away.

'Not bad. He was only little, but he was solid as a rock. Him and his dad watched for a while, then his dad asked if he could play. The boy didn't speak any English, but he didn't really have to say anything anyway. He went into people like a bus! He was really good.'

Chris stood up. He slid the jacket under his arm, folded up into a ball. He leant close to Dave.

'You could still have this lot now, you know. They're bushed. We've run them all over the pitch, and some of them are so unfit they'll still be breathing hard in an hour. Just run them around a bit more, and look for space. Be patient.'

The advice made sense, but Chris could see Dave wasn't buying it. The whole team seemed deflated.

'Sorry,' said Chris, and he turned towards the gate he had entered by. There was only one other choice, and Foster could have reached either easily. It was best not to think about where he might be hiding.

As he went past, Ben was walking back slowly from having fetched the ball. His face was pale, except around the cheeks where there were patches of red. He was sweating too, his thin blond hair plastered to his forehead. He carried the ball under his arm, walking across the grass with laboured steps.

'OK,' he said, puffing hard. 'I think that's it for today.'

Even though he was in a hurry to leave, Chris paused. Along with all the other emotions that were bubbling just under the surface, the fact that Ben was going to abandon the game annoyed Chris in a way he couldn't control.

'You quitting?' he snapped.

Ben didn't read the signs immediately. 'It's getting late,' he explained.

'Sure you're not leaving because we're beating you?'

Confusion and just a little irritation showed on Ben's face at the same time. 'Actually, we're winning,' he said, with a little sarcasm in his voice.

'Not over the last half hour or so,' Chris snapped back at him.

Ben's eyes narrowed, realising what Chris was accusing him of. 'We can beat you, mate! Anytime, anywhere.'

'Yeah?' Chris yelled back. 'I'd like to see you try!'

'Yeah?' his opponent echoed. 'OK, tomorrow, three o'clock!'

They stood there for a moment, eyeball to eyeball. A small light came on in Chris's mind reminding him of the date.

'Christmas Day?'

'Sure, why not? The Queen's speech will be on TV, so the whole country will be asleep. We can play thirty minutes each way.'

'I don't know . . .' Chris muttered, limply.

'Boxing Day then!' snapped Ben, sensing that Chris was beginning to back off.

That really wouldn't work. 'I can't . . .' Chris said, in a low voice.

Ben was smirking widely. Chris looked back over his shoulder, to where the others were watching the argument. His team mates were paying the closest attention.

'Fine,' said Chris turning back. 'I'll be here tomorrow.'

'Uh huh,' said Ben, smiling. 'For a big game like this, we'll use Regent's Park. More room.'

Chris found himself smiling, having very nearly forgotten everything else in the triumph of that moment. OK, he had lied to his aunt about where he was going today; OK, he had stolen a mini-computer; sure, Foster was waiting to catch up with him; yeah, he had just agreed to try and get out of Aunt Helen's flat again on Christmas Day . . .

But that was nothing compared to the mistake Ben had just made.

'Yeah,' agreed Chris, grinning. 'More room. I'll see you tomorrow.'

He took off again at once, trying to get his brain back behind the idea that he was in desperate trouble, but feeling exultant. Yeah, just give me some room to move, mate, and you'll think having nine goals fly past you in twenty minutes was a good result.

He swung open the gate and checked the street. The bright lamps overhead and the glow from the bookshop windows reflected off the pavement, which was starting to show signs of frost. Chris felt the bite of cold air across the back of his neck, and went to pull on the jacket. He stopped himself as he saw a dark car glide around the corner, holding close to the kerb as it came closer towards him.

The only person Chris knew who could outrun a car was the mountie in *Due South*. Chris might have been in with a chance if he had been on Oxford Street, but there was nowhere near the same crowd back here. He took a look at the bookshop, but all its entrances came out on to the same street, so there was no chance to get lost in there.

The car slid to a halt beside him, an electric window sliding down at the back. Chris saw the black hair, then the shades, then the too-clever smile, and finally the sheepskin coat.

'I think you and I should have a chat, son,' said Foster.

⚽

'I'm not allowed to take rides from strangers,' Chris said quickly when the rear door swung open. He was prepared to put up with the fact that it made him sound like he was about six years old.

'Very sensible,' Foster agreed, nodding. He peered at Chris over the top of his shades. Now that the door was wide open, Chris could see that the agent wasn't alone in the car. A young woman in a sparkly dress and what *had* to be a white wig piled high on her head was sitting beside Foster. Right by where Chris stood, there was a huge dark shadow behind the smoked glass of the front passenger door which suggested Tank was squeezed in there.

Snake would be the driver then. If Chris's father's warning about taking rides with strange men ever applied, it was now. They didn't come stranger than this bunch.

Chris took another long look into Foster's dark eyes, which were still firmly fixed on him. He knew what the agent was trying to get him to realise by that long stare. Chris had a lot more to worry about than being trapped in a car with the four of them.

Even so, he didn't move for several more seconds. Then there was a shout from behind him, in the park. The voice was familiar and slightly annoyed.

Chris stepped into the car doorway, ducking his head.

'Move over, Sandy,' Foster sneered to the young woman.

Chris paused, watching her for a second as she wriggled across the seat, leaving space between her and Foster for Chris to drop into.

'Isn't Gloria going to be ticked off that you stood her up?' Chris asked in a soft voice as he fell into the plush leather seat.

The snow-blonde head turned, but Sandy (what kind of name was that for a woman with *white* hair?) had pretty slow reactions compared to Snake, who whipped round sharply in the driver's seat.

'You see, boss!!! He *did* break in. He knows your secretary's name and her name . . .' He flicked a finger towards the young woman at Chris's side, though his eyes stayed fixed on the young man in the middle of the seat.

'Shut up and drive, you idiot,' Foster growled at his employee. 'He probably heard Gloria's name from you . . . and Sandy . . .' He turned to look at Chris, curious to know how Chris had made that connection.

'The phone. Gloria was talking to your . . . friend . . . when we . . . I arrived.' Chris cursed himself inwardly for having reminded anyone that he was just half of the team.

Foster was smiling again. 'You're a clever lad,' he said. 'You have a good eye and an alert mind. It showed in the game back there.' The smile vanished briefly as he signalled to Snake to set off. Snake managed to get the gears in a tangle, and the car stalled. 'Maybe I ought to offer you a job.'

'Thanks,' said Chris, 'but I don't get a lot of free time.'

Foster laughed. 'That's what makes us different. I don't think there is ever a time when I'm not making money. Even when I'm asleep. That's the beauty of what I do. Other people are always making me money. Every minute of the day, someone somewhere is making money and I'm getting a cut.' Chris flickered a small smile back. It seemed a good idea to keep Foster in a good mood. 'Even now. Christmas Eve.' Foster took a look at his watch, a big Rolex with a face that lit up like a torch in the slightly gloomy interior of the car. Chris felt his heart jump as he realised just how late it was getting. He peered through to the front of the car and out through the windscreen, wondering where they were headed.

'A night at the opera, perhaps a meal and –' Foster looked past Chris at the woman tucked in the corner beyond. 'And I still hope to have a very profitable evening. Starting right now. And you can share some of that profit.'

'Oh?' said Chris, his voice almost slipping over the word.

'I'd like to offer you some money, Chris. Quite a lot of money, as it happens. More than I suspect you've seen before.'

Chris offered a sickly smile back to Foster. The words might sound very cozy and the news good, but Chris knew Foster wasn't about to give him anything for nothing.

'First things first,' the agent continued. 'You play a bit, don't you?'

Chris was caught off-balance by the way the question was phrased.

'Sorry?'

Foster laughed, a short bark of amusement. 'Agents are like scouts at first,' he said. 'We have to see something we like; we have to be able to recognise talent. I've been busy in the entertainment industry for years. But I've always loved football, ever since I was a kid. Went to see Millwall play when I was twelve. We lost three-nil, but it was beautiful. The singing, everyone pressed close. And the football. Hard, brutal, but poetic too, you know?'

Chris nodded again. He didn't like to admit it, but he really did understand what Foster was talking about. At least, he had experienced something similar back on that day when Oldcester and Coventry had fought for the right to reach the fourth round of the FA Cup. Every football fan surely had to be able to tell the same story. Even those idiots from Southampton, the ones from the restaurant (an event that seemed a long time ago already); they must have had a day when they watched the Saints play, and from then on they pulled on red and white and dragged themselves all over the country, trying to catch the dream again.

Chris almost warmed to Foster for a moment. Even a Millwall fan could have a heart, surely . . .

'So, I can see when a lad has a talent like you have. Me, I can't play at all. But I know how it should be done.'

He reached out a hand, short fingers wrapped in heavy rings. One stubby digit stabbed towards Chris's shirt. 'Oldcester United. You on their books?'

Chris thought about denying it, but there didn't seem to be

much point. Besides, he wanted to hear what Foster had to say, and then he might just get out of this car in one piece. The Saab had stopped at traffic lights. Snake cracked his knuckles. Chris nodded again.

'Perfect. I knew I could see talent in you. OK, let's talk about proposal number one. You've heard about the little game we have going on Boxing Day?'

The blue leaflet was still tucked in Chris's pocket. 'Sure.'

'It's a charity thing,' Foster explained anyway. 'I set it up to make money for homeless kids, hospitals and things. There's been a bit of needle between a few of the traders on Oxford Street and some people in Soho, so I thought it would be better if it got sorted out on the football pitch.' That all sounded very worthy and innocent. Clearly the story couldn't end there. 'It also gives us an opportunity to let people have a bit of a flutter on the outcome. You know, a bet?' Chris nodded again, trying to assure Foster that he wasn't a complete idiot. 'There's a bit of money involved, and both sides want to make sure their side wins. So, they're both bringing in ringers. Outsiders, you understand?' Chris drew in a long breath, getting impatient. Foster was clearly used to having to explain things to Snake and Tank very slowly. 'When it kicks off, it'll be all under eighteens. The agreement is that there'll be older players after thirty minutes. Free substitution, you know. The last thirty minutes will be all the young blokes. The Oxford Street lads are hoping to get a few pros involved, you know?' He laughed again. 'They've got no chance. They don't have the contacts. It was me that fixed it for the game to be at Brentford, you know. I told them how it would be all kosher, and it will be, as far as they can see! They don't know about the betting.'

Chris shifted in his seat. The car was warm and Foster had a slow, deep voice that was very hypnotic. If he didn't get to the point soon, Chris was going to doze off.

'I'd like you to play for my lads, for Soho. In the under eighteens part of the game. And I'll slip you twenty-five quid if you do.'

Chris thought he knew where this was going. 'You want me to throw the game, don't you?' he said quickly.

Foster managed to look both surprised and a little hurt, which Chris found himself believing was all down to good acting. 'No!!! I want you to play your guts out, and get us a few goals! I want the game to be well in our favour by the time the old boys start coming on.'

Chris tried to read the agent's eyes, but the shades kept them well hidden. There was nothing in the tone of his voice to suggest he was being funny.

'So, how about it? Will you play?'

Chris bit his lip, not wanting to answer one way or the other. Foster waited patiently for a moment, then waved his hand in a dismissive gesture as if he really wasn't that bothered.

'Just think about it. You know where the game is? What time?'

Chris knew. He didn't tell Foster that he had already decided to go, assuming his father could stand the idea of that game as well as the one at the Bridge.

'Just tell any of the stewards at the gate that you are with Laurie Foster's team. They'll show you where to go.'

That seemed to conclude the first part of the discussion. Chris looked outside again. There was some light drizzle starting to fall – in fact, at that moment Snake switched on the Saab's wipers. Chris didn't recognise anything in the street they were passing along, which seemed to be all darkened offices and lunch counters. He saw a direction sign indicating the way to Bank, which suggested they were heading towards the City of London. Wasn't that taking him away from Aunt Helen's?

'On to the second item of business. It has come to my attention that you might be able to help me find a friend who has gone missing.'

Chris tried to look innocent.

'Me? Who do I know in London?'

Foster didn't laugh this time. It had been too obvious a lie.

'You know who I'm talking about. Pavel Davidov. He was supposed to meet me yesterday – in fact, we are supposed to have been meeting up for quite a while. My associates say you saw him yesterday.'

Chris decided not to be at all clever about this. 'Sure. I bumped into him in Oxford Street. Snake and Tank were there, right? Some street weasel stole a woman's purse, and Davidov chased him. I recognised him from the club, of course, so I chipped in to help. We got the purse back, and that was the last I saw of him.'

Foster seemed remarkably interested in the story. His face remained fixed in Chris's direction throughout.

'So . . . you don't know where he is staying?'

Chris shook his head. He genuinely had no real idea.

Foster took a long time before showing he was prepared to accept that as being true. 'A pity. I would have paid you a lot more money for that information. If, by any chance, you did find out before Saturday, I want you to give me a call. If you help me find him, I will pay you two hundred and fifty.'

Wow!!! Chris felt his lips dry as the stakes went higher. Clearly, there was a lot more going on here that he still didn't understand.

'I honestly don't know,' he told Foster. Once again, the agent took his time reacting to the news.

'I'll take your word for that. For now. But I just want to add one thing. There are others looking for the same thing I am. I would be very . . . disappointed . . . if you were to tell them about Davidov.'

Disappointed was a very loaded word in Chris's experience. He had very little doubt that his father was going to be very disappointed when he found out what had been going on.

'I don't understand,' said Chris. 'You're his agent. Why don't you know where he is?'

Chris caught the way Foster glared forward, and he turned his own head so that he could see Snake's face in the driver's mirror. The flunky didn't look very happy. Chris turned back as Foster replied.

'There are some complications in our arrangement that still have to be sorted out,' the agent explained, although it wasn't an explanation that cleared very much up. 'Mr Davidov has certain contractual obligations he needs to be free of.'

Or, put another way, Foster wasn't his agent. He was just trying to jump in on the action, and there were other people in the way. People a lot more scary than Mushy, or even Foster himself.

Foster checked his watch. Chris imagined he was worried about getting to the opera on time. He reached inside the sheepskin coat and took out a thick leather wallet from an inside pocket. Opening this, he pulled out a business card. He closed the wallet and sat with it and the card on his lap.

'The last item we need to discuss involved a notebook I believe recently fell into your possession. There was a great deal of excitement when the owner realised it was missing, and I think he would offer a substantial reward to get it back. So, I'd like to help make that possible.'

Chris nodded. He had been expecting this as the finale. Foster knew Chris had taken the wallet from the restaurant. Perhaps he had even set it up, making sure Chris saw the wallet on his way back from the toilet. By getting Chris to snatch it, Foster had hidden his own interest.

Foster looked at the coat folded on Chris's lap.

'Where is it?' he asked.

Chris took a deep breath, quickly dismissing any idea of being clever. Foster knew exactly how he had got the organiser, and Chris knew he could easily be introduced to the real owner, which wasn't something he looked forward to.

'In my jacket pocket,' said Chris.

Foster grinned. 'I thought so,' he replied. He opened the wallet again, and withdrew twenty brand-new £20 notes. He folded them around the business card.

'All yours,' he said, 'for the contents of your jacket pocket.' He tucked the money into Chris's palm.

'It's a deal,' said Chris, and he handed over the jacket. Foster looked a little surprised, his eyebrows riding up. He lifted it up and patted the pockets.

Chris let him suffer for a moment.

'Oh, that's not mine,' he said at last. 'I must have picked up the wrong coat by mistake.'

Twelve

Chris knew it was a dream when he scored the winning goal in the FA Cup Final. Up until then, it felt like real life. But bending the ball round in a semi-circle from the halfway line, then running to meet his own pass, thundering a volley past his headteacher and being interviewed on the pitch by Des Lynam and Gary Lineker was a bit rich even for Chris Stephens.

The dream began sliding into nightmare when tall men in black suits and old-fashioned hats were waiting in the royal box. As Chris lifted the cup, they brought out machine guns. One of them leant forward and spoke.

'I fink you got sumtink dat's ours, kid.'

Chris tried to run back down the steps, but his team mates were already being mown down in slow motion. The hoods even got Aunt Helen (who'd played a blinder on the left). Another mobster grabbed Chris and started to fight him for the cup.

Finally, Chris started to jump out of sleep, his body jolting upright as suddenly as if the bullets really were striking home. He opened his eyes, realising at once that he wasn't in his own room, then slowly remembering being at Aunt Helen's. And that was when the nightmare got really bad.

'Hey!' said Nicky. 'Merry Christmas!'

⚽

There are times when it's possible to explain problems to your parents. Most of them can be quite understanding, provided they know what caused the incident their little lamb was involved in.

Other times, silence is best. You're in trouble so deep that trying to explain reasons or make up excuses is a waste of time. A quiet 'I'm really sorry!' can cover up a lot of bad behaviour, but you have to time it just right so that it doesn't start them complaining again.

Then there are those occasions when, whatever you say or don't say, it's never going to make things right. From now on, Chris's advice to anyone ever facing that predicament was going to be, 'Don't get caught out on Christmas Day. It can really muck up the whole event.'

There was no easy place to begin to explain the mishaps and misdemeanours Chris was caught up in. It was 7.45am on Christmas morning. For the last hour, Chris had been grilled relentlessly, with just one break when breakfast arrived, served up in silence by Aunt Helen.

'So, where were you yesterday?'

'Shopping,' Chris said. He knew that answer only opened himself up to more questions, but it was at least consistent with what he had told Aunt Helen he was planning to do.

'Until nine-thirty?'

'I got a little lost,' Chris said. 'I ended up walking back here from Tower Bridge.'

It had been a long walk too. After realising that he had been tricked, Foster threatened to throw Chris into the Thames. It had taken Sandy to remind the agent that they needed Stephens to find the real jacket. So, Foster had settled for reaching into Chris's shirt pocket to retrieve the cash he had given him, then dumping Chris out on the approach to the bridge. Chris had no idea what bus or tube to catch, and every cab seemed busy. Chris walked back towards Oxford Street and then followed that along until he got back to the area near Aunt Helen's. The fact that it had drizzled all the way just added to the time it took.

Aunt Helen was pretty frantic by the time he arrived, although she hadn't gone as far as calling his father. When Chris got through the door, she unloaded on him in a big way, reminding him that when he had set off that morning he had been 'popping out quickly' to find a couple of last-minute gifts. Ten hours later, soaked and carrying the wrong jacket, Chris's appearance didn't convince her he was telling the truth.

By the time Chris had eaten and taken a bath, it was getting closer to midnight, and his father arrived. John Stephens reacted to the news even less calmly than Aunt Helen. This morning was more or less an action replay of the night before, with all of the same questions. Not the least of which was:

'OK, so try explaining to me why Nicky is here?'

A witty answer could have been that perhaps there was a guiding presence in the universe, which had created Nicky for some unknown purpose (or that Nicky was just a collection of particles bound together by gravity; a mere coincidence in the flow of time and space). Then again, no-one over the age of eighteen seemed in the mood for witty remarks, so Chris knew he'd have to give a more sensible answer. Whatever that could be.

He and Nicky had tried to talk in the bedroom last night, but Chris's father had stalked in and told them to shut up. So all Chris had to go on was the story Nicky had come out with last night, and which he was repeating this morning.

'I missed my train,' Nicky said, smiling weakly.

'Back up a bit first,' Chris's father snapped back. The four of them were sitting around the small dining table in Aunt Helen's flat. There was tea and toast, and the sound of Christmas carols coming from the radio in the kitchen. That was pretty much it as far as Christmas cheer went.

'Just what were you doing in London in the first place?' Mr Stephens demanded. Nicky flinched under his hard glare. Chris took a moment to see how his team mate was reacting, then turned round quickly as his father switched targets. 'Did you know he was coming? When did this all get fixed up?'

There were a lot of questions to deal with. Nicky could only cope by running through them in order, counting them off on his fingers.

'I came down the day before yesterday,' he said, starting his explanation as far back as he could. 'Chris kind of put the idea into my head . . .'

Chris almost jumped back in alarm. What was Nicky saying?!

Nicky realised that he might be open to being misunderstood at the same moment. 'We didn't talk about it or anything,' he blurted, almost making the sentence come out as a single word, 'but when he said he was staying in London, I thought that would be pretty cool, so I decided to come down as well. You know, see the lights and stuff.' He realised this sounded pretty lame, so he tacked on a last piece of explanation. 'I was staying with Paulo in Hendon – it was all fixed up and everything! I mean, everyone knows where I am. I mean . . .'

Chris could see Nicky was going down fast, so he jumped in to save him.

'Nicky rang me yesterday morning, from the station. We hadn't arranged anything, honest. But I agreed to meet up with him, and we just spent the day up Oxford Street, hanging around together.'

Which was close enough to the truth, Chris decided. He fell silent.

His father remained fixed on Nicky. 'So when did it become part of the plan to miss getting back to Paulo's?'

Nicky's smile turned even more sickly. His face, normally a warm tan colour, like lightly browned bread, was becoming pale green. Nicky rarely got this much grief at home.

'It wasn't a plan!' he responded, just a little too anxiously to be believable. 'I just lost track of time. I missed the train and I couldn't think how to get back there. Hendon's a long way out, you know.'

This was no time for Nicky to show off a newly discovered mastery of geography. Mr Stephens could sense that there were holes the size of Eurotunnel through this version of events.

'You could have rung Paulo and asked him to wait. There would have been another train,' he said.

'I did ring him!' Nicky insisted. 'But it was too late by then . . .' His voice trailed away as he realised this might not have been the best thing to admit. 'Anyway, Paulo said it would make better sense if he came and got me, and I told him I'd wait for him here and . . .'

There were quite a few more ands after that, but Nicky left them unsaid. He had fetched up at Aunt Helen's some time before Chris, explained his story to her, made a few phone calls and then settled down to eat most of the food she had got in for the holiday in a single evening.

To say that Chris had been surprised to see him when he turned up later was an understatement. However, with Aunt Helen shouting at him in one ear, it had been impossible to get any sense of out Nicky about why he was still in London. It was something to do with Paulo losing the address . . . or being given the wrong one.

'So, what happens now?' Chris's father asked briskly, still fixed on giving Nicky a hard time.

'I told my mum where I am,' said Nicky, making Aunt Helen's flat sound like a hotel he had just popped into. 'Uncle Fabian might drive down to fetch me, only the weather up there was diabolical last night.' Mr Stephens narrowed his eyes; was Nicky deliberately forgetting that Chris's father had driven down through the same weather? 'He says he'll check with the AA this morning. If worst comes to worst, I could always come back with you on Boxing Day.'

He finished this remark with his most ingratiating grin, which made Aunt Helen smile back in return. Chris's father had seen it too often to be impressed, though. 'I'll speak to your uncle later,' he said. That appeared to be the end of that.

Mr Stephens turned to his son. 'OK,' he said, 'it's your turn.'

Chris glossed over some of the details of what he had been up to the day before. This had two benefits. One, it got the story out of the way before the new year. Two, it meant he could leave out a few facts that might just have sounded worse than they really were.

On the whole, though, Chris broke the habit of a lifetime and told his father just about everything. He recounted the bag-snatching business with Mushy in Oxford Street, and how this had brought him into contact with Pavel Davidov; he mentioned the reward he got from the old lady, and the top-up from the shop. He tried to back up Nicky's story about how their meeting up on Christmas Eve was a spur-of-the-moment thing, even though this wasn't entirely the truth. He admitted that they had kept an eye out for Davidov, in case they had spotted him, and he told everyone about the football game in the park near the bookstore.

The whole truth and nothing but the truth. Well, OK, he left out a few facts, such as the visit to Foster's office, the encounter with Tank and Snake, the stealing of the organiser and the car ride, but on balance it was a pretty full account. Certainly compared to the usual style of Chris's confessions.

Mr Stephens listened carefully as Chris ran through the day's events and Nicky hoovered toast. The look on his face showed he wasn't buying all of it. Instead, he fixed on the gaps in the story, the parts where it didn't all fit together.

'Why did you and Nicky get separated?' That was easy. Nicky had gone to catch his train, while Chris had wanted to continue looking around.

'What happened to your jacket?' Chris told his father about the football game, and admitted that he had picked up the wrong jacket when he left. He added that he was sure he could find the other guy and swap back. He didn't actually mention the game that had been arranged for that afternoon, but he promised himself that he would. Later.

And so it went on, at least for a few moments longer. Mr Stephens thought of other questions which troubled him and Chris tried to reassure him. In the end, they both knew the whole story hadn't come out, but Chris's father was slowly coming to accept that there might just not be some great conspiracy behind his son's actions.

Not for the first time, Chris bit his lip and tried to deal with the guilt he felt about keeping secrets from his father. The trouble was, he was convinced that if he told the truth, he would be blocked from the appointment he knew he had to keep.

Gradually, the atmosphere thawed, and by the end of an hour Aunt Helen was beaming and nudging her brother with her elbow.

'It doesn't sound so bad really,' she whispered.

'It doesn't *sound* bad at all,' Mr Stephens agreed, 'which probably means . . .'

Aunt Helen wasn't prepared for the gloom to continue any longer. 'Oh, come on, John, you got up to far worse in your time. And it is Christmas.'

Mr Stephens flashed a warning look at his sister that convinced Chris that it had to be worth finding out just what mischief his father had got up to when he was a lad. All the same, the worst was over.

'Fine,' he sighed. 'OK. I'll buy that story . . . for now.'

Aunt Helen almost jumped from her chair, clapping her hands with joy and squealing delightedly.

'At last! Can we open the presents now?'

They descended on the pile under the tree, pulling out

Aunt Helen's neatly wrapped packages and the more basically parcelled gifts Mr Stephens had brought in the car. Quickly reading the labels, they passed them back and forth like demented sorters at a post office for lunatics. Finally, regardless of whether the gift was perfectly dressed in Aunt Helen's shiny metallic foil, with ribbons, bows and bright labels, or it had been bundled into a sheet of cheap paper from a garage, each present was torn open in a frenzy of excitement. It was like watching sharks at snack time.

At first Chris wondered why Nicky was involved, save that the hilarity was catching, but then he realised Aunt Helen had wrapped some chocolate and other stuff while they had been asleep, just so Nicky had some paper to tear as well.

There weren't vast numbers of presents – certainly not compared to the mountain that swamped the Fiorentini sitting room – but everyone had tried to make an effort to be generous and thoughtful this year. Aunt Helen was delighted with the perfume Chris had bought her on his father's advice, and even happier with the cassette of choral music Chris had thought of himself. She had bought her brother a really excellent jacket with an embroidered picture of Taz on the back. Chris was about to suggest he might borrow it, but then realised this would bring up the missing baseball jacket again. The glass ornament appeared too, and everyone laughed when Nicky blurted out how all the others were locked up in a cabinet, and then tried to pretend he had been talking about some other house.

Chris got some excellent software for the Mac from his father, plus some jeans and the new Dodgy CD. He showed it to Nicky; one less album he would have to borrow from the Fiorentini library. There was other stuff too, including something from the club which Chris agreed not to open in front of Nicky, since the same gift would be waiting for him at home.

Amazingly, there was even stuff from Nicky to Mr Stephens and Aunt Helen. Chris sighed and closed his eyes, knowing what they had to be. Just as he dreaded, the adults pulled out two of the appalling Christmas novelties Nicky had purchased the day before. Aunt Helen actually thought her 'Ho, Ho, Ho' Santa was cute. Nicky beamed delightedly.

Finally, Chris opened Aunt Helen's present to him. She

looked worried as he took off the paper, and started confessing that she hadn't known what to get him, especially now that he was playing football all the time for the club, but she knew how it was *so* important to him and . . .

It was a football. A good-quality Adidas match ball. Aunt Helen looked more anxious than ever as Chris checked it out. His father must have told her that the ball he kicked around at home was showing signs of all the punishment it had taken. Chris looked up. He could see Nicky's face, which reflected what he must be thinking (Like we don't see enough footballs, eh, Chris?). His father waited for him to say something.

'This is great, Aunt Helen,' Chris began, and then his face cracked open into a genuinely happy grin. 'This is just about the best present you could have got me.'

Thirteen

Escaping from the flat was easier than Chris ever imagined.

'These guys are playing football on Christmas Day?' Mr Stephens asked, placing another of the breakfast dishes on the draining board.

'I expect they just want to get out of the house for a while,' said Chris. He had done it himself last Christmas, scooting round to Nicky's to play FIFA '97. A year or two before, all the Spirebrook football mafia had gone to Memorial Park for a game against their hated rivals from Blackmoor. In the true spirit of Christmas, they had thrashed their rivals 8–3 and then taunted them until their goalkeeper had split Nicky's lip.

Chris didn't mention that latter story to his father.

'So, I was thinking, Nicky and I could go to the game, maybe join in, and I could get my jacket back.'

'Good idea,' Mr Stephens added, and Chris had just a few moments to congratulate himself before his father added, 'I'll come along.'

So, at about 2.30pm, with the Christmas turkey in the oven and everything else peeled, sliced and ready for cooking, Chris, his father, Aunt Helen and Nicky stepped out of the door of Aunt Helen's flat, turning north on to the Edgware Road and then following the Marylebone Road to the park.

Chris and Nicky walked just ahead of the two adults. Chris had the new ball in his arms, and they were both wearing their Oldcester shirts and jogging bottoms under their coats, along with several other layers of clothing to protect them against a raw easterly wind that blew hard into their faces.

The word was that the weather up north was even worse. Not a white Christmas, just a grey one, with blustery winds and driving rain. It hadn't taken long to persuade Uncle Fabian that Nicky was better off where he was.

There weren't a lot of people out on the street. A few dog walkers huddled against the chill gale, while some brave souls were trying to walk off early dinners. Mr Stephens was extremely doubtful that anyone would turn up for the game at the park, and Chris felt pretty much the same.

Still, it was the best chance they had. In fact, it was the only chance he had of meeting up with Dave and the others and getting his baseball jacket back. Not to mention . . .

'I don't get it,' Nicky said in a quiet voice as they battled the wind.

'Don't get what?' Chris replied.

'Foster,' Nicky said, allowing his voice to drop so low it was hard for Chris to pick it up. It wasn't that dangerous a word, but Chris looked over his shoulder in alarm anyway. Luckily, Mr Stephens and his sister were gradually dropping back, talking about old times. Chris had been trying to earwig, in case they said anything about the tricks his father had got up to as a boy. Information like that could be really useful.

'Foster wants me to give him Davidov and the organiser, and for me to play in this charity game,' Chris said. 'It sounds pretty straightforward to me.'

Nicky glared at him, as if Chris had just said something pretty dumb.

'That's just on the surface,' he said. 'You have to dig deeper.'

Chris burrowed his head into the collar of his borrowed coat. At times like this he knew Nicky could keep talking for hours.

'If he's Davidov's agent, then how come Foster doesn't know where he's staying?'

The same thought had occurred to Chris several times. He was pretty sure he had the answer. 'I don't think he *is* Pavel's agent,' Chris explained. 'But he wants to be. He probably thinks there's a lot of money to be made from having a Premiership player on his books.'

Nicky wasn't buying into anything that simple. 'You need all sorts of permission and stuff to be an agent,' he said. 'From the FA. I don't think Foster's got any of that.'

'Maybe it's not the football side he's interested in. Perhaps he wants to handle all the sponsorship and other stuff.'

Nicky couldn't bring that argument down, but he didn't show any sign of accepting it either. 'Too simple,' he said. 'I reckon he has other plans.'

Chris frowned as he caught the satisfied smile on Nicky's face, which was Fiorentini's patented 'I've got it all sorted' smile. Once again, he checked behind to see that his father and aunt were now even further back. They were looking in a shop window, sharing a joke.

'Like what?' he asked irritably.

Nicky's smile vanished. Clearly, he hadn't been expecting to have to reveal the workings of his devious mind. Perhaps he thought Chris had been keeping up.

'Match fixing,' Nicky said in a hushed voice.

Chris almost yelled his surprise out loud. Nicky was accusing Pavel of being involved in chucking games? In Chris's books, there was no worse crime. Fans stood in the wind and rain, paying a fortune to see their team give everything they had for a result. It was bad enough when your idols played below form – Chris remembered how frustrated the Southampton lads had been after the whipping the Saturday before. But the idea that a player could deliberately throw a game away, that was impossible to describe. It was spitting in the face of his team mates and 20,000 fans.

'Nicky, since Pavel arrived, we haven't lost a game. We've barely let in a goal. What you're saying –'

'It makes perfect sense,' Nicky anticipated. 'The people behind this, they're waiting for a big game. Maybe like the one against Chelsea tomorrow. Or the games up at Anfield and Old Trafford at the end of the season. It could decide the Championship, it could . . .'

Chris shook his head. He didn't believe it. He didn't *want* to believe it. 'That can't be it, Nicky. Why Davidov? Why would Foster pick on him out of all the players in the League? You have to have something on someone; you have to know they're dirty *before* you can try asking them to throw games.'

Nicky followed that reasoning silently for a moment, which was a relief. Up ahead Chris could see the entrance to the park, and the tall trees swaying in the gusting wind. He was sure Nicky was wrong. All the same, the match at the Bridge suddenly seemed a lot bigger.

'OK,' said Nicky abruptly, 'the other bloke then, the Russian bloke whose organiser you borrowed.'

Chris knew at once who and what Nicky was talking about, and it caused an empty, tight knot in his guts. 'We don't know he's Russian,' he began.

Nicky's face twisted in mockery. 'Oh, come on, you said the stuff in the organiser was written in Russian,' he scoffed. Chris warned his mate to be quieter. Nicky took the advice, but didn't let go of the subject. 'Well, didn't you?'

'How should I know?' Chris hissed, contradicting the info he had given Nicky before his father had shut them up last night. 'It was foreign, with funny letters. Could have been anything!'

'In the circumstances, it's hardly likely to have been Peruvian or Indian or something, is it?'

Chris decided against picking Nicky up on his knowledge of foreign languages. His point was quite accurate.

'OK, the notes are in Russian,' Chris conceded, 'but that doesn't make the guy Russian, does it?' Nicky opened his mouth to protest but Chris beat him to it. 'After all, we've heard him talk. He didn't sound foreign.'

Nicky took a moment to think. He had paid the guy so little attention on either of their two previous meetings, it seemed very unlikely that Nicky would remember the organiser's owner having two heads, never mind that strange accent. On the other hand, he wasn't so sure now that the guy was English. He certainly did speak in the most unusual way.

'So who is he then?' asked Nicky.

Chris didn't answer. He couldn't have supplied one just then anyway, but even if he had been trying to speak, the words would have died in his mouth.

A figure darted out of the doorway on his right, moving very quickly. Chris had barely noticed him before the man bumped into him hard. He had the impression that hands quickly felt both the pockets on the borrowed coat, then the ball was prised from his hands. He turned round quickly, with a cry on his lips.

That brought him face to face with the guy, who had bounced half a step away. At once Chris took in the dark, sweaty face with the thick black beard and the dark, rapidly shifting eyes.

'Mushy,' he breathed.

The bag thief and hustler flashed his eyes at Chris, looking both frightening and frightened. The ball was held between his hands, which were clad in fingerless woollen mitts, and shaking violently.

'You have something of mine!' he snarled, his voice giving a kind of nervous hiccough at the end. Chris took that half step towards him, but Mushy jumped back again, holding the ball like it was a kind of hostage.

'What are you talking about, Mushy?' Chris growled back. Looking past the street thief, he could see his father and Aunt Helen closing the gap between them. Mr Stephens hadn't really caught on that anything strange was happening yet, but he was looking in their direction.

'You know what I mean!' Mushy squealed. 'You've been following me for days! Who are you hoping to sell it to? The Russian? You'll get nothing there, kid, except trouble.'

Chris could see his father was very close now, and had recognised that something was wrong. Anything Chris said now would be overheard, so even though there were questions queuing up to be spoken, he bit his lip and forced them back. Mushy would have to keep.

'I have no idea what you're talking about,' Chris said very loudly. 'You'll have to get your own ball!'

Mushy looked back at him as if Chris had gone mad. Chris had the same worry about the street rat. Mushy looked very rattled, even more so than he had when Pavel had lifted him off the floor. He looked at the ball he was cradling in his hands, and a wide grin spread across his dark features.

'Ahhhh!!!!' he yelled. It started off as a cry of understanding; it ended up as a squawk of surprise.

It was almost possible to feel sorry for Mushy. Every time he thought he'd found a nice easy target, things went wrong for him. Two days ago it had been Davidov who had robbed him of a bag; today . . .

The ball bounced loose. Chris bent and picked it up, then looked back at Mushy who was gurgling gibberish as he squirmed in John Stephens' grip. Chris's father had one arm locked round Mushy's neck, the other fist clamped on his hand, a carbon copy of the way Davidov had worked the trick in the Harvester.

'Get your own ball, son,' snarled Mr Stephens, then he flicked Mushy to one side, so that the thief pitched over a pile of black plastic bags outside a cafe. He hit the pavement with a loud slap, then dragged himself upright. He started to yell some threat, but Aunt Helen cracked him around the shins with her boot as he ran past and Mushy went down again.

'Ow!' laughed Nicky. 'Red card tackle.'

Mushy fled away, the odds way too much for his liking. Chris and the others watched him go.

'Maybe Santa will bring him a ball of his own next year,' said Nicky grinning, 'if he's good.'

Chris and his father exchanged a long look, and Chris knew Mr Stephens suspected there was much more to this than some poor mad crook with a desperate need for a football. Then he looked at his watch, and realised they were almost late.

Nicky wanted to talk as they walked along, but Mr Stephens was much too close. Besides, Chris needed to think. Something was beginning to make sense in his head, and, for once, it had very little to do with football.

Fourteen

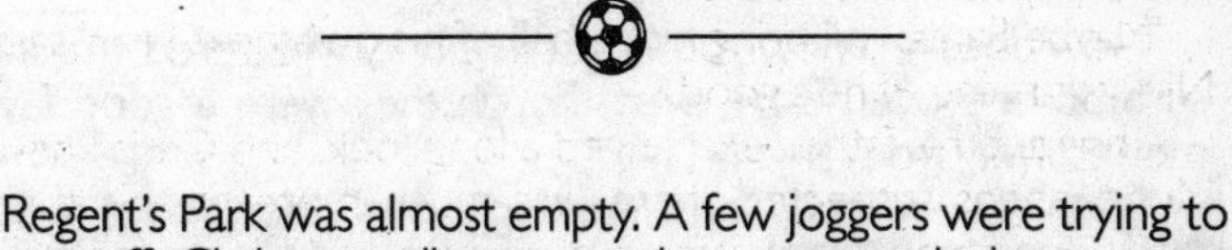

Regent's Park was almost empty. A few joggers were trying to run off Christmas dinner wearing vests and shorts, even though the wind had come all the way from Siberia. Most of them looked ready to drop dead on the spot.

Chris was amazed at how large the park was, and it took a while to track down the game. His father was about to suggest they forget the idea when they saw some boys milling round on a flat square of grass on the eastern side of the park. One of them was wearing a baseball jacket.

Chris breathed a sigh of relief and started to trot over. His father's voice pulled him back before he had taken more than a few steps.

'We're leaving before it's dark, OK?' Mr Stephens insisted. It wasn't up for discussion.

It was almost three already, and even though the sky was clear over in the west, the early night could be no more than an hour away. Chris nodded to show that he agreed to the condition – he had no great desire to be out after dark anyway. If Mushy could find them, so might Foster, or anyone else for that matter.

He and Nicky started to run across the grass, but then Nicky slowed him down. Chris looked around at his team mate, wondering what this interruption was for.

'What was Mushy talking about?'

Chris shrugged, and turned his attention back to the group of kids. There seemed to be a few missing from yesterday's cast. Those who had braved the cold wind were gathered around one of the makeshift goals, mostly familiar but with a lot of new faces as well. Several of the replacements seemed to be gathered around Ben, who had his cheap plastic ball under his right foot.

'Ben's brought along a few mates,' Chris said, announcing out loud what was foremost in his mind at that moment. Then he recalled Nicky's question. 'I'm not sure, but I think it has something to do with the organiser.'

Nicky's face showed that he was thinking the same thing, even though neither of them was quite sure how it all pieced together.

'How does he know you've got it?' Nicky whispered, making sure no-one overheard, even though they were a good few metres away from anyone.

'I don't know,' said Chris. 'And right now I don't have it. So first things first, OK?'

'Hi, Chris!' came a voice from the middle of the pack ahead. Chris looked round and saw Toby running up to meet them. There was a moment of alarm when Chris realised that Toby wasn't wearing his baseball jacket – had Chris been mistaken? – but then he saw it was already on the top of the pile being used to mark out one of the goals.

'Hey,' Chris said, breathing a sigh of relief. 'This is Nicky, a mate of mine.' Toby and Nicky exchanged brief nods and mumbles of greeting.

'We can use the help,' Toby admitted. 'Mickey and Joseph aren't here, and Ben has brought along some mates to add to his team.' Chris could see the new arrivals, lads of Ben's age. There was nothing about any of them to suggest they had any talent; they were standing around looking cold and fed up, as if they had been forced into playing.

The losses on Chris's side weren't critical, although they would miss the presence of Mickey's backside if there were any goal-line chances. Joseph, a big, slow-speaking lad from Ghana, had kept goal for them in the other game, so there was a brisk discussion going on about who should take his place.

'We've just been arguing if it's fair for Ben's mob to have two extra players when we were two short,' Toby continued.

'Don't worry about it,' Chris told him confidently.

Toby's face didn't express a great deal of confidence. Chris looked round his team mates, pointing out a few individuals to Nicky. They decided that a barmy, loud-voiced lad named Luke should go in goal, simply because he had an Arsenal shirt on. Then Chris noticed a new face among their group.

'That's the guy I was telling you about,' said Dave, grinning. 'His name's Potty. He can't speak English, but he's a brilliant player. Just stick him in the middle of defence and we'll be solid back there.'

Potty was a smallish lad, although he looked the kind who could be a real bruiser when he grew up. His face was square and pale, with sharp grey eyes and closely cropped blond hair. He seemed bright enough, and when Chris signalled to him to play at the back, the lad nodded and smiled, flashing a set of tiny white teeth with a single gap at the top. Chris wondered who had been foolish enough to knock that tooth out, and just how badly they had paid for it.

He turned to Toby. 'Sorry about the mix-up with the jackets,' he apologised, trying hard to be sincere. Toby smiled weakly. As Chris dropped the dark blue jacket he had 'borrowed' on to the pile, he thought about checking to make sure that the wallet was still in the pocket of his own coat. However, that would look really untrusting. It was bad enough that, side by side, the two jackets looked so completely different. There was no way Chris could have mistaken Toby's for his.

He tried to put it out of his mind. The 'mix-up' was all behind them now. Chris could see his father standing nearby with Aunt Helen. He pointed down at his jacket and gave a thumbs-up. Mr Stephens nodded. All might not be forgiven, but at least Chris had proved one part of his story to be true.

'So, you're back?' came a new voice.

Chris turned to face Ben. 'Hey . . . ready to start?'

'Ready to lose?' Ben came back, grinning confidently.

'We'll have to see if we can remember how,' Nicky broke in. There was nothing he liked better than a bit of needle, and he and Ben were made for each other.

'You'll remember. In fact, why don't we have a little bet on the game, just to make it interesting?'

Chris's team mates looked at each other nervously. They had been on the wrong end of too many beatings to like the way this idea sounded, plus they were intimidated by the sheer size of Ben and his mates. Nicky, on the other hand, was already digging in his pockets.

'I've only got a quid and a bit,' he told Chris, knowing which of them had all the money for a change.

'Is that all?' mocked Ben. 'Haven't any of you other little boys got any money?' He fished in the pocket of his jeans and pulled out three ten pound notes. 'I've got thirty quid here. Can't you lot come up with that lot between you?' There was complete silence. Chris could imagine how his side felt about that kind of money.

'Stop waving it around!' he snapped.

Ben laughed. 'What's the matter, kid? Don't you get pocket money? Frightened you might lose?'

Chris knew what Ben was trying to do. Every bully in the world tries the same thing. 'Go on,' they say, 'have a smoke. What's the matter, are you frightened?' Chris had learnt a long time ago not to get sucked in. There were plenty of other ways to pull his chain, but trying to make him out to be a coward wasn't one of them.

However, something made him act differently this time.

'I just don't want my dad to see, OK?' he snapped back. He slapped Ben's hand down, then quickly pulled out some of the money he had collected over the last few days. It was growing into quite a tidy sum. Chris had counted it again this morning – £30 from the old lady, another £35 from the shop – and had been amazed when it came to £85! One of Foster's twenty pound notes must have been left behind in his shirt pocket when Chris was thrown out of the car.

'I'll cover your bet,' he whispered. 'We play to four o'clock, no later, OK?'

Ben grinned broadly, then turned back to his team mates. He slapped hands with one in particular, one of the new boys. 'This is Phil,' he announced. 'He's had a trial with Fulham!'

The smile faded just a little when he heard Nicky giggle.

'Shut up,' Chris hissed at his team mate. He faced Ben again. 'I've brought a decent ball this time.'

'Suits me,' shrugged Ben. 'Winner gets to keep that too.'

'Fine,' said Chris automatically. He stepped away and gathered his makeshift team together to explain their gameplan. It didn't take long. The others were looking very sheepish.

'Look,' said Toby, sounding extremely embarrassed. 'I'm not sure the rest of us can help with the bet –'

'Don't worry about it,' Chris said without any trace of emotion. 'I've got it covered. Win or lose, it's down to me.' He gave each of them a hard stare, trying to gee them up. 'Just make sure we win, OK?'

⚽

Fulham must have been flush for decent players to have passed on Phil, because he was a good midfielder. A bit of a David Batty type; determined, hard-tackling and very competitive. He won Ben's team a lot of ball.

His passing was OK, but he was let down by the fact that the two key players on his side – Ben and another older lad – expected the ball played to feet all the time. Phil wanted to hit angled crosses so they could exploit their height advantage, or through balls they could run on to. His team were only interested when the ball came directly to them. In addition, their first touch was usually poor, as if the cold had sapped their concentration. And that assumed that they got a first touch.

Though he barely came up to their shoulders, Potty snapped away at the forwards like a Rottweiler on steroids, giving both of them an early opportunity to taste the grass. He gave away two dangerous free kicks that way – one of which ended up in the goal – but they looked a lot less keen to take him on afterwards.

The trouble was, there were two of them, and just the one Potty. Phil used his eyes and brain, and started playing passes to whichever of them was furthest from the bullet-headed defender. No-one else on Chris's team could tackle that well. Toby, who had been up front alongside Chris, went back to lend a hand, but even he was struggling for size against the older lads.

Crazy Luke was kept very busy. He had a lot more enthusiasm than skill, though, and goals leaked past him every couple of minutes.

It was the same problem Toby, Dave and the others had faced in all the previous games – Ben's lot were too big to stop, and they could score almost whenever they liked. The only difference this time was that Chris was keeping his mob in the game.

With all the opposition's big lads up front, Chris had a lot more room to make chances at the other end. The extra space on the bigger pitch and the fact that they were using a better ball helped too.

For every two goals Ben's team scored, Chris scored one himself. Ben reorganised his team, and tried to shut Chris out of the game. However, with a little help from Dave and a lucky deflected goal from Toby, Chris's efforts kept the score close by half-time.

'Twelve-nine,' gasped Toby. 'We're doing pretty well.'

The others agreed, although Chris noticed they were all avoiding eye contact, worried about how they were just a half-hour short of costing him £30. Everyone looked winded, but Chris could see that Ben's team was breathing even harder, especially Ben himself. The air above them was clouded with plumes of vapour.

'OK,' Chris said quickly, as his team mates huddled around him. 'Change of plan. If you get the ball, don't pass to me, pass to Nicky.'

This caused a small murmur throughout the team. In the first half, Nicky had stayed wide, marked on and off by one of Ben's younger players. He had played very little part in the game.

'Trust me,' said Chris.

The others slowly nodded to show their agreement. Then Chris made one last tactical adjustment. 'Potty,' he called.

The blond lad looked up from the soles of his boots. He pointed at his chest. 'Pyotr,' he replied. Chris gave him a quizzical look, then listened hard as the kid repeated it. Pea-ot-ear. Chris felt a small buzz of recognition. 'Pyotr,' the boy said again, tapping his shirt.

Chris took a longer, harder look at the kid's replica shirt. It was a striped affair, with a central badge. Chris fixed on that.

Pyotr looked down, following the focus of Chris's eyes. 'Dinamo,' he said, and the word came out with a thick, rolling accent behind it. 'Dinamo Moscva.'

Chris's face opened in a wide smile. 'Oh, yes,' he whispered. He patted Pyotr on the shoulder, then turned to point out a player on the opposition team. He held up his hands, fingers upright. 'Pyotr,' he said, indicating his right hand with a small wave. Then he shook the other hand: 'Phil.' He checked that the small defender was watching carefully, then moved both hands close together.

Pyotr nodded and grinned his missing-tooth smile once more. 'Nu ladno,' he replied. Chris wasn't definitely sure that meant 'OK', but it certainly sounded like it.

'Toby, cover the back to start with. Potty's going to move up into midfield. If things go to plan, push up as the half ticks on. Ben and his mates look done in. I don't think they'll give you much more trouble.'

'None of us is that fresh either,' Toby pointed out.

'Oh, I don't know,' said Nicky. He and Pyotr were grinning at each other like idiots.

Chris got to his feet and moved forward. Ben was lining up, ready to kick off again.

'Hey, Ben,' Chris said calmly, patting his pocket. 'Let's make it fifty quid.'

The other boy looked back at him, and there was just a little nervousness in his eyes. 'You're kidding, right?'

Chris grinned as well now. 'What's the matter, Ben? You frightened?'

Fifteen

'Jingle bells, jingle bells, jingle all the way; Oh what fun it is to see Ben's team lose away, oh . . .!'

Dave had started singing about three minutes before the end. By the time Nicky got his fourth goal, a wicked curving shot that the goalkeeper had dived *away* from, the whole team was joining in.

Chris held up his watch. 'I make that three minutes past,' he said.

Ben looked sick, but there was no point arguing. Chris's father had called in just before with the same kind of time check. And besides, his shattered team were 22–14 down.

Chris stuck out his hand. 'Nice game,' he said, smiling.

Ben looked at the open palm and his face clouded over. He reached into his pocket very, very slowly, then pulled out the money he had brandished earlier. It almost hurt him to slap it into Chris's palm.

'I'll have to get the rest from the other lads,' he said in a miserable, low voice.

'Fine,' said Chris. 'Give it to Toby. Our lot can split it up.' He looked around quickly to see if his father was watching, but Mr Stephens and Aunt Helen were walking around the back of one of the goals, talking with a man and a woman who had come along to watch the second half.

Chris pocketed the thirty quid, then held his hand out again. Ben's face turned pale.

'I said I don't have it! I'll give it to your mate Toby, OK?'

'I know, I trust you,' said Chris as soothingly as he could. 'But don't you lot shake hands after a game?'

Ben hesitated, then shook Chris's hand. 'You and your mate are pretty good. We'd have had the rest of this lot easy.'

'I know,' said Chris. 'That's rather the point, isn't it?' He couldn't help smiling. Everything was falling into place.

Ben didn't have a clue what Chris was driving at, and walked away to join the rest of his sullen team mates, who were collecting their coats and trudging off along the paths through the deserted park. Toby and the others were in the middle of the pitch, their joyful voices echoing all over the deserted space.

'That went well,' said Nicky, walking over. He had been singing as loud as anyone.

Chris grabbed him round the neck and messed up his hair. 'Better than you think,' he replied. 'That's how it's done.'

Nicky tried to look up, but couldn't. 'That's how what's done?' he squawked from somewhere down under Chris's armpit.

'How the game Foster has organised is fixed. It's not about throwing a game, it's about winning one. Thanks to a ringer. You know, a player brought in to outclass the other side. Or more than one, in this case.'

Nicky was silent for a long moment, and Chris had to check that his mate had got the plot. 'I get it . . .' Nicky said at last, his voice distorted.

Chris laughed. 'Come with me, I have a surprise for you.'

Nicky followed (not that he had a lot of choice while he was in a head lock) as Chris made his way towards the goal. His father was chatting with the guy who had turned up, a tall man with dark curly hair who was the spitting image of his kid. The man had already picked up Toby's blue jacket, the one Chris had mistakenly borrowed after the other game. As Chris watched, his father tugged his baseball jacket up from the floor by the loop inside the collar. Chris's heart missed a beat, but Mr Stephens did no more than drape the jacket over his arm.

The mix-up appeared to be the subject of conversation. Both the men were looking at the two jackets, wondering how anyone could have been stupid enough to mistake one for the other. Chris decided not to join in.

Instead, he swerved towards Aunt Helen, who was talking to the woman who had arrived. She was tall and very pale, with long blonde hair spilling out from under a black fur hat. She wore a matching coat, trimmed with fur, that reached down to the tops of her black knee-high boats. She was very elegant, and just a little nervous, or so it seemed to Chris.

Her son was loitering in front of her, laughing and trying to break into her conversation in a babble of foreign words. When he saw Chris walking over, Pyotr called something over to his team mate, and laughed even louder.

'Hey, Pyotr!' Chris called back. The two women turned to face him. Chris released his grip on Nicky and walked the last few metres to join them. 'Hello, Mrs Davidov,' he said.

⚽

It would have been very embarrassing if Mrs Davidov hadn't understood him, or had pretended not to (there was never any doubt in his mind that it *was* Mrs Davidov), but Chris's words had their desired effect. The elegant woman's eyes opened very wide.

'You're joking . . .' Nicky whispered.

Aunt Helen was impressed with Chris's knowledge too. 'You know this lady?' she asked.

Chris couldn't claim that exactly, so he said nothing. Instead, he kept his eyes on Mrs Davidov, who was looking around as if she was waiting for someone or something else to arrive – a nuclear missile, perhaps.

'It's OK, Mrs Davidov,' he said. 'I'm a friend. I know your husband.' He pointed at his (grubby, by now) shirt.

'Oldcester,' said Pyotr, grinning, and he pronounced it just the same as his father could do, with all the extra Rs at the end.

Mrs Davidov didn't look all that relieved at the news. 'How did you know we would be here?' she asked. Her accent was as rich as her husband's, but her English was just that little bit better. Her eyes glittered as she spoke, flitting about from side to side.

'I didn't,' Chris explained. 'I saw your husband the other day, so I knew you were in London, but I didn't know you would be coming here today. When I spoke to Pyotr, I just worked it out. Pavel said you were both arriving in England before Christmas.'

Mrs Davidov had listened carefully to everything Chris said. A little of the fear in her eyes disappeared. All the same, she looked very keen to leave the park and get back to whatever hiding place she was using.

Chris spent a long time thinking about what to say next.

'Mrs Davidov, is your husband with you? I mean, is he still here in London?'

'Yes,' the tall woman said at last. She glanced at Aunt Helen, who reached out and gave her a consoling touch on the arm. Mrs Davidov relaxed a little more. 'At least he was. We have been staying in a hotel. But Pavel has gone out today. I do not know when he will be back.'

Chris smiled, and nodded. They were so close. 'We know he has a problem,' he said. 'We'd like to help. I'm sure we can help you sort out whatever it is.'

That probably didn't sound as convincing as he hoped it would. Mrs Davidov looked on the brink of tears, as if the pressure of the last few days was about to catch up with her. Chris didn't have the slightest idea how to deal with such a crisis.

'I cannot,' she replied. 'Pavel says we must not let anyone know where we are staying.'

Aunt Helen tilted her head sympathetically to one side. 'There, there,' she said softly. 'Not much of a Christmas Day for you, is it, in some lonely hotel? Look, why don't you come with us. We'll go back to my flat and have a nice cup of tea, and maybe a spot of dinner.'

Nicky giggled, as if the idea struck him as stupid. Chris watched Mrs Davidov pull Pyotr closer, as if she was thinking of fleeing, then slowly relaxed.

'Please, yes,' she said. 'I would like that.'

Chris managed to prevent himself from punching the air in triumph, or banging heads with Nicky in the way they normally celebrated a goal. It looked as if things were finally heading their way at last.

Chris watched as Aunt Helen led the Davidovs off towards the Marylebone Road. Nearly everyone else had gone too. He could see Toby and his father in the distance, almost disappeared from view. Ben and his mates had also left.

He turned round, ready to collect his jacket and set off back to Aunt Helen's flat. His moment of exultation shattered in that same moment.

His father was lifting the black leather wallet from his pocket, pulling it out into the open. The look of surprise on his face matched the one that Chris was starting to wear as well.

'What's this?' Mr Stephens asked.

'That? Uh . . .' Chris began. And then all he could think to add was: 'Merry Christmas.'

⚽

It would have been hard for things to get much worse, but fate tried its best. Someone had sloped off with the new ball.

⚽

Dinner was going to be wonderful. Aunt Helen had really done them proud. The turkey must have won weight-lifting medals at the Olympics and the stuffing was home-made; a chestnut, sage and onion mixture that was just right. There were potatoes, brussels, carrots, Yorkshire puddings, small sausages, twists of bacon, small lemon and onion balls and several litres of gravy.

For afters, there was pudding, in brandy butter and a light cream, mince pies and chocolates. Even though they had two unexpected guests, there was plenty of food for everyone. Nicky said it was just like being at home, only without anyone singing opera.

Mrs Davidov gave Aunt Helen a hand in the kitchen, getting extra vegetables peeled and cooked. Chris volunteered to help too, but his father didn't let him escape. Nicky and Pyotr watched TV, so there was no help to come from that quarter.

The subject of the pre-dinner chat was obvious. Chris sat at the dining table opposite his father, the black leather wallet between them. Mr Stephens had unzipped it and looked the organiser over. He hadn't turned it on yet, which was a blessing. Chris still had a little time.

'Where did you get this?' his father asked.

'Down here in London,' Chris admitted.

'Chris, these things cost a fortune. We sell a cheaper model in the store. Even with my staff discount they cost a lot of money.'

'Well,' laughed Chris nervously. 'I could hardly come and ask you to get one for yourself, could I?'

His father smiled a little, turning the machine over between his fingers so that the keys were upmost. 'Where did the money come from?' he asked.

'I got all of it while I was down here,' Chris explained, and he then went into details about the rewards he had received for his part in capturing the bag snatcher. Chris just managed to avoid calling Mushy by name.

'I'd say that still left you short,' Mr Stephens insisted.

'I had some other money, savings . . .' Chris offered, lamely. He was suddenly very aware of the fortune he had stashed in his pocket.

His father nodded, looking the machine over. His thumb passed over the on-switch several times, which made Chris's heart beat faster.

'You'll have to take it back,' Mr Stephens said at last.

'What? Why? Don't you like it?'

'It's too much, Chris. Plus, look. It's worn here on the surface. Probably not a new one at all – it's a demo model or something.'

'Really?' said Chris, his voice catching in his throat. He leant over so he could pretend to notice the small marks on the casing.

'You do still have the box?' his father asked.

Ah. Chris made a small noise of discomfort, looking around the room as if a box might magically appear.

'You did get it from a shop, Chris? Don't tell me you bought it from a street trader! Helen told me about some of the sharks who were operating Oxford Street this year – is that where you got this?'

Chris couldn't bring himself to speak. As all parents are trained to do, Mr Stephens took this to mean the answer he was dreading. For once, this wasn't such a bad thing.

'You idiot, Chris,' his father snapped. 'For all you know it could be stolen.' Chris managed to start an answer this time, even if all he managed was a strangled 'Urk!' It took Chris a moment to work out that his father wasn't accusing *him* of having stolen it (which really would have been unfair). Meanwhile, Mr Stephens was aiming a finger at the on-switch. Chris's next words tumbled out.

'You're right!' Chris cried out. 'I was stupid. I'll take it back. The guy might be there tomorrow, right? So I'll nip out and see if I can find him in the morning. Get my money back.'

Mr Stephens narrowed his eyes and gave Chris a long stare. 'Wouldn't it be better if I came along?'

'My mistake, my problem,' said Chris. 'I'll deal with it.' He grinned at his father, aware just how false it must appear. 'If I don't have any joy, you or Aunt Helen can have a go at him later.'

He held his hand out for the organiser. His father took a long while to hand it over.

'Maybe we should take a look,' Mr Stephens said cautiously. 'Just to see if it might have been stolen.'

'I don't think so,' Chris said hurriedly. 'I mean, there's no data on it. I checked.'

Mr Stephens considered this fact for a while (Chris prayed that he wouldn't take a look for himself). He was still in favour of checking with the police.

'That'll take for ever, Dad. Let me try and sort it first. I'll get the money back and then . . . and then . . .'

'What?'

'You could buy yourself one with your staff discount,' Chris said.

⚽

'You were lucky there,' Nicky whispered, without looking away from the cartoon. He and Pyotr were like twin statues, side by side on the carpet in front of the screen, their faces bathed in the vivid colours of the desert where Wile E Coyote was getting trashed by the Road Runner.

Chris sat down beside his mate, heart thumping. He had the organiser on his lap. 'This is getting out of control,' he admitted, looking down at the stolen object. 'I have to get rid of this.'

Nicky reacted in alarm. He clearly thought his partner was talking about dumping the organiser in the river.

'I'm talking about getting it back to its original owner,' Chris explained in a low voice. His fingers ran along the leather case. 'If I don't give it back, this thing is going to get me into a lot of trouble.' He thought about what he had said for a moment, and then added: 'A lot *more* trouble.'

Nicky turned away from the TV for a moment. 'Have you worked out who the original owner is?'

Chris looked up at once. 'What?'

Nicky was already facing the screen again. An explosion painted his face red and white. 'I'd give it to Foster. He's as likely to be the original owner as anyone else, plus he'll give you money for it.'

Chris could see that might make sense in Fiorentini world.

He wasn't convinced. 'How could it be Foster's?' he asked, allowing his voice to creep up in volume to get Nicky's attention.

Nicky shrugged. As far as he was concerned, the compelling argument was the money. The person who needed it most was the one who offered the most money for it. Obviously.

'It's got notes written in Russian,' Chris reminded him. 'That means it can't be Foster.'

'How do you know?' asked Nicky. 'He might speak the language, or he might have had someone at that restaurant write the stuff for him.'

Chris wasn't convinced. 'You could say that about anyone we've met. It's not very likely, though, is it? And how many people do we know who speak Russian?'

Nicky smiled, and flicked his head towards Pyotr, as if proving his point. Chris groaned loudly.

'What we really need,' he said after recovering his composure, 'is someone who could read this thing for us. Somewhere, it might say who it belonged to, or the notes might give us some clue.'

Nicky nodded to the side again. Pyotr was giggling loudly at the coyote's latest demise. Chris realised what his partner meant, and frowned. 'Nicky,' he whispered, 'what's the point of asking someone to translate who can't speak English?'

Nicky's face lit up as he realised that was a good point. He grinned stupidly and pushed back his hair. 'His mum, then,' he whispered, with a glance towards the kitchen door.

It was a better suggestion, but no more practical. 'There's no way we can ask her to translate this stuff without telling her what we did to get it. I'm not sure that would be such a good idea.'

Nicky agreed, and turned back towards the TV, where the cartoon was coming to a close. Wile E was making one last desperate attempt to catch the dumb bird. Chris knew how he felt. This whole business with Pavel Davidov was a puzzle that seemed so easy, and yet always remained out of reach.

The key to it all was the organiser. Chris had stolen it from the mysterious man who had been following them, the guy they had seen first in Oldcester, and then later in Oxford Street. They had heard him speak, and he didn't sound

Russian. Maybe Nicky was right; maybe it belonged to someone who could speak the language.

Who else? Well, there was Mushy. Surely there was only one way to understand that scene in the street. Mushy wanted the organiser. In fact, he seemed to think that it belonged to him. What was it the bag snatcher had said? 'Who are you hoping to sell it to? The Russian?' Who did that mean? Pavel? The only other Russians Chris knew (excluding Mrs Davidov and Pyotr, for obvious reasons) worked at the Odessa restaurant. Chris didn't consider them 'suspects'. On the other hand, the manager had warned Chris about the 'Mafia'. Now that he thought about it, Chris remembered snatches of stories on the news about the Mafia in Moscow. Perhaps he could ask Mrs Davidov about it . . . or maybe not. Whoever 'the Russian' was, it couldn't be Mushy himself, nor the guy Nicky kept crossing swords with.

So who did that leave? Foster? Again, from everything Chris knew, Foster was neither Russian nor spoke the language. But he wanted the organiser so much he had set Chris up to pinch it for him. And he was trying to pull some kind of scam at the charity game, that was certain. Chris was pretty sure he had that worked out, but he couldn't see where the organiser came into it, and he couldn't see why Pavel was in Foster's pocket.

So, if the organiser was the key, which lock did it open? The mystery just seemed to get deeper and deeper.

Chris pulled the mini-computer from its case and flipped it open. He wanted to take another look at the address book, just on the off-chance there was a name somewhere that would help identify the owner. He thumbed the switch.

Nothing happened.

He gave the machine a few seconds to wake up, then flicked the switch on and off again. Still nothing. He turned it over and opened the hatch at the back, and saw that there were batteries in there, the new kind with the on-cell tester. They seemed fine.

Chris thought about using the adaptor, but he knew that power wasn't the problem. A terrible dread crept over him.

The cartoon was over and the credits were rolling. Pyotr looked round with a delighted grin on his face, and saw what Chris was holding for the first time. The grin vanished at once.

'*Mat!*' he yelled, leaping to his feet and pointing. He rushed out into the kitchen, still shouting, '*Mat, idi syuda!*'

'What's all that about?' Nicky asked.

Chris felt his sixth sense start to scream like an alarm siren. Pyotr returned, pulling his mother into the room by the hand, which meant 'idi syuda' probably meant 'Come and make things really awkward'. Mr Stephens peered around the kitchen door to see what was going on.

Mrs Davidov didn't seem to understand all the fuss at first, but slowly Pyotr got her to take a close look at the leather wallet Chris held in his lap. At once her pale grey eyes widened, and she lifted one hand to her mouth. It took her several moments to find breath to speak.

'What are you doing with that?' she asked. 'It belongs to my husband.'

Sixteen

Apart from being in more trouble than he had ever known in his life, and in danger of being grounded until the Millennium, Chris was feeling pretty good. Almost.

For one thing, he had just taken a giant leap forward in understanding what was going on. And, in the back of his mind, cogs were turning as he cooked up a plan that would solve the whole mystery once and for all.

However, just for the moment, Mrs Davidov was sitting at the table, holding the organiser in her trembling hands. Pyotr sat at her side, looking worried. She was in a state of shock already, so Chris hadn't yet told her that the machine was broken. No point making life any harder.

He was opposite her, his elbows on the table and hands clasped as if he was praying. Perhaps that wasn't such a bad idea. His father was standing behind him with his hand on Chris's shoulder, so running away to join the Foreign Legion wasn't an option. This was probably for the best, all things considered. Chris's French wasn't that good either.

Nicky was sitting beside Chris, listening intently. Aunt Helen called from the kitchen. Dinner was just a few minutes from being ready.

'You say this belongs to your husband?' Mr Stephens asked.

Mrs Davidov shook her head and answered 'Yes', which was a little confusing. Then she quickly added, 'I mean, yes, he has had it for a while, but it doesn't belong to him.'

Everyone took a moment to get more comfortable. It appeared this could be a long story.

Mrs Davidov took a long, deep breath and plunged right in. Now that the truth was starting to appear, it poured out in a torrent.

'Back in Moscow, Pavel was in trouble. He was in debt. He

borrowed a lot of money to make sure we were able to live during the bad years, when the Russian economy collapsed. He was in the second team at Moscow, you understand? The wage was not enough to live on.' She took a moment, then continued. 'Plus, he had some other debts. Gambling. Nothing very serious at first, but added to the rest, it made things worse. But when he started to play first-team football, it seemed things must get better. But no. I didn't understand, but then Pavel told me. He owed a lot of money to some bad people. Criminals. He had been gambling, and had lost a lot of money.

'Then Mr Parkes came to see the club, and offered to buy Pavel's contract. Pavel was happy, Dinamo were happy. It seemed like a chance to make a fresh start. But the Mafia were not happy. They said Pavel must pay his debts. They said that when he came to England, they would appoint an agent, someone to tell Pavel what to do. He must pay back the money he owed them, and be prepared to do them favours.'

Chris said nothing, but his excitement was growing. Coupled with what he had been told at the Odessa, this started to make everything clear.

'Pavel knew what that meant. They would ask him to fix games. They would ask him to make Oldcester lose. He couldn't do this; he told them that he would not betray his team. They did not listen.

'So my husband took a big risk. He stole this machine from one of the criminals. It has all the records of Pavel's debts on it, plus the names of other people who also owe money. Important people. Other footballers and sportsmen. Government people. Pavel thought he could keep the organiser, and that if the criminals came looking for him, he would threaten to give the information to the newspapers.

'They did not like what he had done. So, when Pavel came to this country, they bribed officials to make a mess of my papers, so I had to stay behind. That was a little warning, to make Pavel nervous. And then an agent appeared, who said he wanted to make Pavel rich. We didn't believe it; we thought he was from the people back home.

'Pavel reminded this man about the organiser, but he did not go away. Pavel told him he would go to the police, to the newspapers, but this man would not listen.'

'Who is he, Mrs Davidov?' Chris asked gently, trying not to interrupt too strongly, but anxious to know for sure.

'His name was Laurie Foster,' Mrs Davidov replied. Chris smiled to himself. Of course, that was how Foster had got to hear about the information in the electronic notebook – in his panic, Pavel had told Foster himself.

'Then, another man came on the scene. He said he was a journalist from a German newspaper. He offered to buy the organiser. He called Pavel on the telephone, hounded him. He came to the house in Oldcester. Pavel told him to go away, but he would not. The man insisted. He said someone was coming from Moscow to take the organiser back and to get their money. Pavel told him again: "Go away!".' The man followed him everywhere, and even started speaking to people Pavel knew . . . He spoke to Mr Lively at the club. Everyone!'

It was all coming together. Chris knew the 'journalist' had to be the guy he and Nicky had bumped into twice.

'After the Southampton game, Pavel went home and found that the organiser had been stolen while he was out having dinner. He knew Pyotr and I were on our way to join him, so he came to London to meet us. We had to think what to do next. Pavel was contacted by the Moscow people – they wanted their money back.'

Chris listened, feeling a great deal of sympathy for the Davidovs, and a little guilt. Pavel had stayed away from home because he had been in the Harvester with Chris and Nicky, chatting and joking while the organiser was stolen. Maybe that was why Chris's name was in the notebook – someone must have thought he was a decoy.

'He was sure they had the organiser once more,' Mrs Davidov continued, 'so he agreed to do whatever they said. They said he was to meet their agent in London; someone called Illyana.'

That was a name Chris hadn't heard before. He wondered if Illyana might be someone connected to the Odessa. It didn't seem likely that it could be someone Chris didn't know at all. Whoever it was had organised the burglary in Oldcester, which was a neat trick. Or had they? How had the organiser then ended up in the hands of the German?

'When was all this?' Mr Stephens asked. Chris looked up. At

least this was a simpler question than the ones he had been running through.

'Two days ago. Pavel left the hotel to go the meeting at the Odessa restaurant. Illyana showed him the organiser and said that he must do as he was told. Then Pavel saw two of Mr Foster's people and got worried. He and Illyana left the restaurant. On Oxford Street, a man bumped into Illyana and took the organiser . . .'

'Mushy,' said Nicky, who was keeping up with the plot pretty well. He was writing notes on a pad of A4 paper, of course.

Chris felt his father's hand close on his shoulder a little more tightly, and knew he would have to explain how Nicky knew that name later. Great . . .

The name didn't seem to mean anything to Mrs Davidov, since she continued with her story. 'My husband chased the thief and caught him . . . with the aid of a young boy.' She looked up at Chris. 'You, I take it.' Chris nodded.

Mrs Davidov thought about that for a moment, then continued. 'They recovered Illyana's bag, but somehow the organiser had gone missing.'

Chris played through the incident in his mind, trying to work out if there was any way Mushy could have hidden it while he was running. It didn't seem likely. As far as Chris could tell, Mushy hadn't even had time to look inside. It seemed highly unlikely he would have known the value of an object that he had never heard of. At the same time, he had gone to a lot of trouble to snatch that particular bag – stealing a near-identical one from the old lady in the shop, then singling out Illyana and presumably making a switch after he had 'bumped' into her. Pavel must have seen it happen and given chase.

So, who had ended up with it after the chase and Mushy's capture? Illyana? Chris presumed Illyana was the young woman who had followed Davidov along the road. If she had recovered the machine, then she would have continued to work on Pavel as before. Davidov, then? Again, that didn't make sense. If Pavel had got his hands on the organiser, wouldn't that have been the end of his problems?

What about Foster? Snake and Tank had been on hand, but how could they have known about Illyana? How could they have found the organiser? And besides, Foster didn't have it later. Mystery man did.

Which left Mushy. But how had he known the notebook even existed? How had he known to sneak it out of the bag before he was caught?

Chris could see Nicky was writing questions on the pad. Chris really felt like he wanted to add another 30 or 40 of his own. Far from providing all the answers, Mrs Davidov's account was making him feel even more troubled.

'Pavel was sure he could forget Illyana now that she didn't have the organiser. All the same, he did not think we could leave London either. Mr Foster was still demanding to see him, and we saw the German journalist at the Odessa, asking questions. Pavel did not think we could trust him.'

The same guy who Chris and Nicky had seen with the organiser the next day. How had it got back to him? Chris was sure the Davidovs were right not to trust the guy – he must have been the one who stole the organiser originally. After all, he'd had it in The Wanderers, when Nicky first bumped into him.

So, if he'd ended up with it on Christmas Eve, didn't that mean he'd set up Mushy to nick it the day before?

Mrs Davidov's story finally came to an end. She didn't know anything about what had happened over the next few days. Foster and his goons had been looking for them; the German and Illyana were still around too. Then Foster had tracked them down somehow, and called the hotel. He said he had the organiser, and wanted to make a deal. Pavel had gone off to meet him.

Mrs Davidov's head dropped forward, as if telling all this had exhausted her. 'But you had it all the time, Chris. You had it. How is this possible?'

Once again, Chris felt his father tighten his grip.

'I think you owe everyone an explanation, son,' he said firmly.

Chris looked up to see his father's face set sternly. He sighed. Finally, he looked across at Fiorentini.

'Start a new page, Nicky,' he advised his team mate. 'I think we're going to need it.'

⚽

'You've still got a lot to account for, Chris,' Mr Stephens said, his voice just a little slurred. 'But more than that, you'd better have some plan for putting things right.'

Chris said nothing, although he was wondering if he would be forced to do any of this extra explaining that night. After running through the whole story once again (well, almost the whole story; there were still a few details he had kept to himself), Chris had almost lost his voice. However, after a complete Christmas dinner, a couple of glasses of wine and half an hour in front of the TV, Chris could see his father was gradually drifting away.

There was a slim chance that Mr Stephens wouldn't remember all the details come the morning, which might just allow Chris to escape being grounded until Oldcester next won the cup. Chris was trying hard not to worry about that now. There were more important things to deal with first.

Nicky kept looking at a list on the piece of paper in front of him, running his hand back through his hair over and over as if he was trying to wake up his brain cells with the friction.

'Pavel took the organiser in Moscow . . . then someone, probably the German, took it from him. Illyana got hold of it somehow; Mushy got it from her in Oxford Street and gave it to the German. Then . . .' Nicky dropped his voice. 'You got it from him, lost it to Toby, then got it back.' He dropped his pen at the end of what had sounded like a *Match of the Day* commentary for a complicated attack. 'So who does it belong to?' Chris shrugged.

'Does it matter now anyway?' Nicky continued, thinking out loud. 'It's bust. So whatever was on there is lost and Pavel can't use it any more.'

Nor could anyone else, Chris thought. That didn't seem like such a bad idea, but at the same time he knew it didn't do the Davidovs any good.

Then a thought popped into his head from nowhere.

'Mrs Davidov, you say your husband went to see Foster?'

'That's right,' Pavel's wife replied from the other side of the room, where she was sitting in one of the armchairs with Pyotr asleep on her lap. 'I should go soon. He might be back at the hotel by now.'

'Well, we can find that out,' said Chris, and he pulled a crumpled business card from his pocket. 'May I use the phone, Aunt Helen?'

Everyone caught the confident note in his voice. They all knew this meant Chris was working on something (even Mrs Davidov, who had only seen him in action this one time). His father watched closely as Chris went to the phone and dialled.

'Mr Foster? We met the other day, and you gave me your card. You were looking for Pavel Davidov and –' He paused, looking round the room. Everyone was listening. 'He's with you? Oh. So I guess you don't need my help with that any more then.

'OK, there was that other thing you wanted. Yeah, that's right. Well, I've got it. Uh-huh. So, you still want it? OK. Only there are some other people after it too, you know. OK, OK, just checking. That's fine. And you still want me to turn up for this charity game of yours tomorrow? OK. I'll be there. Yeah, and I'll bring the organiser. OK, bye.' He dropped the phone back on the cradle. 'I'm afraid Pavel isn't going back to the hotel tonight, Mrs Davidov, but he'll be going to the game tomorrow with Foster.' He could see the look of alarm in her eyes. Chris smiled brightly. 'Don't worry . . . I think I have a plan . . .' he said.

It was unlikely that Mrs Davidov was reassured by the prospect of a teenage boy rescuing her anyway, but when she heard Nicky and Chris's father moan loudly, she must have wondered just how much trouble she was really in.

Seventeen

That Saturday morning was bright and clear – definitely the best day of the holidays. The damp, cold wind of the last few days had died away, and the sun shone pale but bright through a few high, wispy clouds. An overnight frost had cleared and it was actually quite mild.

All told, the perfect winter day for a game of football.

There were a few people loitering around Brentford's ground, but most of the soccer supporters Chris saw on the streets that morning were making their way to Stamford Bridge, early arrivals for the big clash between two of the top three in the Premiership. Foster's charity game was going to be lucky to attract more than a few hundred people.

Chris yawned as he made his way towards the ground. It had been a long day already, and there was still a lot to get through. He shifted his bag into a slightly more comfortable position on his shoulder and made his way towards the turnstiles.

The first person he saw was Tracy, the girl from the charity shop. She saw Chris at the same moment, and shrieked an ear-splitting 'Coo-EEEE!' that threatened to break windows and shatter eardrums for a mile around. Chris waved back, then tried to duck out of sight.

Immediately, he saw someone else trying to keep a low profile – Mushy, loitering on the corner, was talking to a few very shifty-looking individuals. When the street rat caught sight of Chris, his face clouded over. He stepped away from the group surrounding him and closed the distance on Chris, scratching at his beard.

'Get out of my way, Mushy,' Chris said in low, level voice.

Mushy grinned and barked a short, cruel laugh. 'Is it in there, then?' he asked, nodding at the bag.

Chris could see the naked greed in Mushy's eyes. It frightened him, but he wasn't going to back down. He ignored the question and moved to walk past. Mushy lifted a hand to stop him.

'Don't do this, Mushy,' he whispered.

'The German's prepared to offer a lot of money for that organiser,' the dark-haired thief said, his lip curling. 'And there you are, all alone.'

'Not alone, Mushy,' said Chris. 'There are plenty of people keeping an eye on me. And do you really want Aunt Helen to beat you up in front of an audience?' He swept his hand round, as if indicating that Helen was close at hand. Chris knew that although the ratty little man liked to talk tough, he was really a coward. His eyes opened wide at Chris's words, and he looked around nervously at the people milling around near the entrance.

'And here's a thing,' Chris continued. 'What are you doing working for a German? I thought it was a Russian you were worried about.'

'Germans, Russians, they're all the same thing,' Mushy hissed. 'You'd better not be trying to stitch me up.'

'I could never stitch up a fellow Palace supporter,' said Chris, grinning.

Mushy gave him a blank stare. 'What are you on about? I'm from Oldcester. I'm a United man.'

'I know,' said Chris sadly. 'It just goes to show, doesn't it?' He looked closely at the bemused thief. 'Believe me, Mushy, you'll get what's coming to you. Now where do the players go?'

Mushy gestured vaguely towards a painted wooden door in the nearby stand. As Chris walked past him, he could almost feel Mushy's eyes locked on the bag, trying to guess what it contained. Chris hitched it again, and carried on walking.

Almost at once, there was another familiar face in his way. It had appeared out of the thin crowd as if by magic, as if the owner had been sheltering behind someone, waiting to pounce.

'The boss wants to see you,' sneered Snake.

Chris choked on a comeback about how Foster could pay his entrance fee like everyone else, sighed, and turned to follow the greasy-haired flunky towards a familiar car parked just along the road. Snake's earring jumped and jingled as its owner walked cockily ahead of Chris. For the first time, Chris noticed that it was designed from lots of little silver snakes entwined around each other. Very attractive.

Tank was standing at the rear door, and managed to remember to open it without further instruction. Chris peered inside. Foster and his young companion in the wig, Sandy, were sitting on the back seat, as if they had been cruising around that way since they had dropped Chris off. Foster even looked the same – he had a jacket and tie on under that appalling camel-coloured coat. Sandy was in jeans and a heavy sweater, with a large purse on her lap.

They were sitting much closer together than before, so there was no room for Chris to get in between them. The reason for this was immediately obvious. Sitting on the far side, head bowed to keep from cracking it on the roof, was Pavel Davidov. Chris gave him a small smile. Pavel did not return it.

'Hello again, son,' said Foster, beaming. 'Good to see you! All ready for the big game? Going to give Mushy's mates a good hiding, are we?'

'How should I know?' shrugged Chris.

Foster was full of good cheer this morning, his smile wide and beaming. It was made all the more jolly by being surrounded on the one side by Pavel's expression of misery and on the other by Sandy's look of complete boredom.

'Of course! Of course!!! Who have the traders got playing for them? Some local kids, a few shopkeepers and a couple of no-hopers from the bottom division of the local league. Then look at my team. I've got you, I've got Pavel Davidov –' He turned to give Pavel a pat on the arm, as if they were old mates '– and a few other lads who will be more than good enough to give the traders a walloping.'

'Maybe Mushy found a few ringers too,' said Chris.

Foster laughed. 'I'm sure!!! All that talk about Teddy Sheringham and Vialli – the great dope never even checked to see if Chelsea were playing!'

Foster really was disgustingly pleased with himself. As soon as he could stop laughing, he added: 'I tell you, I stand to make a pretty penny on some of the bets I've covered on this game. Plus, I have Pavel signed up for all kinds of deals. Things couldn't be brighter!'

Chris took a moment to get his head clear and focused

before he spoke again. 'Pavel might not be such a big asset if you make him play. You realise that he'd be breaking his contract with United by playing for you.'

Foster waved his hand as if swatting an annoying fly aside. 'United!! A bunch of no-hopers with no money. No, what Pavel needs is a decent contract with a decent team. So, if United are stupid enough to let him go, that suits me. I'm sure we could get him into one of the big clubs.'

That was what Chris had suspected. Once Foster had his claws into Pavel, he'd be able to force the big defender to do anything he liked.

'And all this comes about because of this stupid organiser?' Chris asked, and he lifted the bag a little, to show where it was.

Foster's greed showed through his eyes. He laughed again. 'That's right, son. There's a lot of power in the words written in that thing. And it belongs to me.'

Chris managed a small smile of his own.

'Not yet,' he said. 'There's a small matter of some money . . .'

Foster's mouth opened even wider. It was a wonder he didn't crack his face. 'You're a lad after my own heart, kid. I've got your money! Just hand over the organiser.'

'Money first,' said Chris. 'Out here.'

He took a step back and put his bag on the floor, unzipping it. Foster pushed out from between Pavel and Sandy, and stepped heavily from the car, reaching into his coat pocket.

'What did we agree, son? Four hundred?'

Chris nodded. 'But you only owe me three hundred and eighty. One of the notes got stuck in my pocket the other night.'

Foster seemed to find that quite amusing. 'Honest! I like that! Never you mind, lad. That was my mistake, and I believe a man should always pay for his errors. Four hundred I said, and four hundred I meant.' He opened his wallet, which was stuffed full of cash. He counted out eight £50 notes, folded the bills and held them out to Chris. Chris looked at the wad of notes for a long time.

'And twenty-five for playing, you said.'

This time Foster almost killed himself laughing. 'Honest and demanding!' he said when he had recovered his breath. 'A rare combination! Here!' He handed over the whole lot. Chris's hand was shaking as he took it.

'One thing,' he said, as he pocketed the cash and reached into his bag. 'I'm just curious how you came to know this thing existed. And how come you ended up with it in the first place.'

The voice that came from behind him was rich with that familiar Lloyd Grossman accent, over-pronounced English rolling off the tongue as if the words were large sweets, blocking the guy's mouth.

'Perhaps I can explain.'

Chris stood up quickly. He wasn't entirely surprised by the new arrival. After all, everyone else was here. But he hadn't heard the guy creep up. Nor, it seemed, had anyone else. They were all looking at the leather case Chris had in his hand.

'Herr Koln,' said Foster, saying the guy's name with a big, fake German accent. 'Good of you to come.'

The newcomer didn't look pleased to be there. He stood stiffly at Chris's back, his hand almost trembling, as if he was tempted to try and make a grab for the case.

Foster leant forward. 'This gentleman is a journalist from Germany,' he said in a quiet voice. 'He's the one who told me about the organiser originally. He's working on a story to expose some Russian crooks; that suits me because the Ruskies have been sticking their nose into all kinds of things round here. Anyway, he'd heard I was trying to become Pavel's agent, and thought I might be able to persuade him to hand the gadget back. I decided to lend a hand more directly.'

'You broke into Pavel's house?'

'No!' chuckled Foster. 'That would be illegal. I just knew a man who might.' Snake giggled at this information and, a moment later, Tank joined in. Smashing a window seemed about their style, Chris thought. One more piece of the puzzle filled in.

'Then I gave the gadget to Herr Koln, up in Oldcester,' Foster continued. 'After all, he paid me good money for it. However, before I handed it over, I made a copy.'

That really was news. Chris had never considered that possibility.

He looked up at the German. 'So why were you so keen to get your hands on it?' he asked.

'Because it's mine,' Koln answered firmly. 'The organiser belongs to me.'

That grabbed everyone's attention. Even Foster stopped smiling.

'You're –' he gasped.

'That's right,' Koln said, without waiting to hear what he was. 'I am Russian, not German, and I deal in money, not newspaper stories.'

Foster turned to look back into the car, where Pavel was easing himself out of his seat to join the small throng on the pavement. Looking past Koln, Chris could see Mushy was sliding over, looking to join in the fun.

'Is this right?' Foster asked Pavel, quite horrified.

Davidov and Koln looked each other in the eyes. 'I'm afraid so, yes,' the footballer said slowly.

Chris watched the stand-off. Suddenly, it seemed like a good time to be somewhere else. However, he knew he couldn't leave until the whole thing was clear in his head, and he had got Pavel off the hook somehow.

'My, my,' said Foster. 'You have been clever.'

Koln grinned. Chris remembered how often Nicky had tangled with the guy and it almost made him laugh. Fiorentini would be speechless when Chris told him he had been gobbing off to a Russian hood!

'So, you stole the organiser from him . . .' said Chris, pointing first at Davidov and then at Koln.

'. . . you stole it from Pavel . . .' This bit was aimed at Foster.

'. . . and gave it to him,' back to Koln. 'Only you copied the data on to another organiser first.'

'That's right,' Koln agreed, wearing a slightly edgy smile. 'The only thing Foster didn't know was that I have a safety device built into the programme. When the data is copied, the original is wiped clean. That way only one copy can ever exist.'

Chris's mouth opened and then closed again. A shiver ran up his spine.

Foster was filling in the gap. 'Sorry about that, Koln. I

didn't really want the data for itself, you know. Just as leverage over Davidov here. I had no idea about your little security device.'

That news didn't exactly make Koln look any more forgiving.

'You had to get it back again,' said Chris, trying to get used to the new gameplan. 'So you asked –'

'Me!' announced Mushy, proudly. He stepped up to join the circle of men on the pavement. Shorter and so much dirtier than any of them, he looked even more the odd one out than Chris.

'Ah, yes . . .' Foster said. 'Gloria informed my associates that I had told her to take Pavel and the book to Tottenham Court Road tube station. And on the way, her bag was snatched . . .'

'. . . Pavel managed to grab Mushy . . .' Chris added.

'. . . but I had already done a switch with the bags!' Mushy concluded, proud of his achievement. 'And you were so hung up on that, you never noticed I had already stolen the organiser.'

Chris knew that wasn't quite the truth. Pavel had slipped the wallet to Mushy after he told Chris to go away. He looked across at the big defender, and he knew why at once. He'd let Mushy disappear with the notebook because it would have to be easier to get the computer back from him than to get it away from Foster. And he had no idea that Mushy and the German were working together.

'So you told Gloria to take it to the station?' demanded Foster.

'No, not me,' Davidov said, with a shrug of his big shoulders.

'You, then?' Foster asked Koln. He shook his head too. Foster fell silent. 'Then who . . .?'

'Does it matter?' asked Koln. 'The fact is Mushy brought the organiser back to me, for which he was richly rewarded.'

'Not that richly,' Mushy broke in. Koln flashed him an angry look. Mushy muttered something more about how no-one appreciated the risks he'd run. Koln snapped at him to shut up. Foster was asking Snake and Tank if they knew who Gloria had been speaking to. Mushy moved around behind Chris to accuse Foster of trying to take over some other crooked operation he'd set up. Everyone was babbling to everyone while, almost in the middle of the ring, Chris was left holding the organiser, and working the rest of the plot through in his head.

From Mushy, it had gone to Koln, and Chris had taken it from him. That might make his father less inclined to be angry, if he ever really found out about that episode. 'Hey, Dad, I didn't steal it from anyone who didn't deserve it, just from the Russian Mafia.'

Foster had run out of patience. 'OK, none of that matters now. The fact is, the organiser belongs to me. Hand it over, kid.'

'Think carefully,' said Koln, glaring at Chris with his electric blue eyes.

Chris hesitated. 'Sorry,' he said. 'Mr Foster paid me for it.'

And with that, he handed the organiser over.

Foster's gleeful smile returned. He stepped away from the ring towards the car. Tank and Snake moved up protectively.

'Wait,' he said suddenly. 'How do I know this is the real thing?'

'Check it,' said Chris.

Foster didn't need to be told twice. He pulled the machine from its wallet, flipped it open and keyed it on. Chris saw him look through the notebook.

'It's in Russian,' he said.

'What did you expect?' said Chris.

Foster grinned. 'Just checking, kid. That proves it is the real thing.'

'And if I'd copied it,' said Chris, 'you know that the original would have been wiped.' Judging by the way his lips spread even wider, Foster hadn't worked that out for himself.

'Excellent,' he said. 'I think our business here is concluded. Pavel, Chris, go and get changed. It's time for Mushy to get his second beating of the day. And in the meantime, I'll just take this somewhere safe.'

He got back into the Saab, chuckling happily. 'Sandy, my dear,' he said, 'it looks like we'll be celebrating tonight!'

Snake jumped into the driver's seat, sneering at those they left behind. The car slid away, engine purring. Chris and the others watched it go. Chris clenched his fist tight, the nails digging into his palm. This was no time to start laughing.

'You just made a big mistake, kid,' said Koln, drawing himself up to his full height.

'I don't think so,' said Chris.

'You're wrong,' said Koln. 'That information you gave Foster is very damaging to me and my associates. We have plans to invest some time and money in London, but Foster will be in our way. He has already been very difficult over our takeover of the Odessa restaurant. And you should have considered Pavel Davidov, here. Foster will control him now.'

'Instead of you.'

Koln dismissed that idea with a shrug.

'Our only interest in Pavel is that he should clear his gambling debts. I don't see any future in controlling a player at a team like Oldcester.' He said the name mockingly. 'What is the point of throwing games with a team who are likely to lose all the time anyway?'

Chris was almost ready to argue, but decided against it. Team pride could wait for another day.

'So, if he can clear his debts, you'll be through with him?'

Koln shrugged. It wasn't much of an answer, but it was as good as Chris was going to get.

'OK, then,' said Chris. 'I'll make you an offer. The organiser for the debt. I give you one, you cancel the other.'

Koln's eyes widened. Pavel looked suitably surprised too.

'That price might be a little high . . .'

'I don't think so. It gives you a head start with Foster. Plus, he need never know. After all, it's not like he can check whether the information he has is genuine, can he?'

Koln didn't understand straight away, but as Chris explained, a light came on in his mind.

'That wasn't *the* organiser.'

Chris smiled.

'But he checked it. He said it was good. And if it was a copy, the original would be wiped clean.'

'What he saw was Russian,' said Chris. 'Doesn't mean it was your Russian.'

'Ah!' said Koln. His eyes glittered greedily. 'You had help . . . from Mrs Davidov, yes?'

Chris nodded. It had been a rush, getting to the shops first thing to buy the second organiser, then getting Mrs Davidov to put in some names, addresses and other notes. She had still been typing as Chris put on his jacket and listened to one last warning from his father.

'Half the debt,' said Koln, interrupting Chris's memory. They both looked at Pavel, who nodded once. From what Chris had been told by Mrs Davidov, that still left a sizeable chunk to pay, but he knew that Oldcester would help Pavel get clear of the rest. Plus, they could find him a Gamblers' Anonymous group so that he never got started again.

'Done,' said Chris, and he reached down into the bag.

'Oh-oh,' he whispered.

Koln bent forward as well, looking into the bag. The only thing visible was Chris's kit. The Russian crook thrust his hand in and moved everything around, but there was nothing else in there but Chris's Oldcester United shirt, some jogging bottoms, socks and trainers.

Koln came upright again, glaring at Pavel for no good reason, turned to face Chris, and then kept turning rapidly to look for –

'Mushy!' gasped Chris.

The bag thief was already 30 metres away and disappearing fast, scattering people as he went. From where Chris stood, it looked like he had something tucked under his arm.

Koln uttered a cry of rage, clenching his fist. He spun round to face Chris as if expecting him to go off after the prize.

'Hey!' said Chris, raising his hands. 'He's not my partner.'

Koln said something in reply, which sounded very rude even though Chris couldn't speak Russian. Then he took off after Mushy. Having seen the bag thief run, Chris was pretty sure a 50-metre start was more than enough for Mushy to disappear in streets he knew a lot better than Koln did. All the same, the bigger man went off after him at a good pace, and they disappeared around the corner about eight seconds apart.

'That still means we've paid off half the debt!' yelled Chris as Koln turned the corner. He wasn't sure if Koln heard him, or if he'd see things the same way even if he had, but it felt good.

A few seconds later, there were just Chris and Pavel Davidov on that part of the pavement, looking off down the street at the people on the corner who were cheering and laughing at the disappearing chase.

'Who do you think will win that race?' Pavel asked after a while.

'I don't think it matters,' Chris replied, grinning.

Pavel thought the same thing, but in a more gloomy way at

first. But once Chris told him what either of them would find if they tried to turn the organiser on, he cheered up quite a bit.

'Well,' he said, 'what do we do now?'

'Well,' said Chris, 'as I recall, we have a game of football to play . . .'

Eighteen

'Come on, get back!!' yelled Chris. In his head he added, Five more minutes, that's all you have to hold out.

The blues came out of defence again. Their midfield tried to string passes together while bringing the ball forward, but none of them really had the skill to make anything clever happen, so the dark-haired midfielder settled for hoofing it upfield again.

A sizeable proportion of the crowd off to Chris's left cheered loudly: 'Forza Paulo!' The guy waved back, smiling. Chris knew that the fact that he was the spitting image of a dozen of them had more to do with their applause than the quality of the pass.

The blues had a bloke up front with long, wispy blond hair and a pair of Doc Martens on his feet. He was tall, he could jump, but it really wasn't a fair contest. For about the twentieth time, Pavel Davidov just leant forward and headed the ball away.

'Yes!' Chris yelled, laughing. He checked his watch again. The ref had already played about six minutes of injury time. By now, even the players on the blues team were looking at him and pleading that they'd had enough. Mushy's mate, Benny, limped over and had a word with him.

'So, who wins the bet if it's a draw?' asked Aunt Helen.

'I don't know,' Chris admitted. 'But it won't be Mushy and it won't be Foster. Maybe they'll have to have a replay or something.'

'By which time it won't be our business,' his father said firmly. Chris gave him no argument.

Chris looked off to his right, away from the chanting Italians and off towards a small group of people sitting quite apart from the rest of the crowd. They didn't look happy.

Snake kept bending down to whisper something to his boss, but he got waved away. Tank had been sulking since his boss had shouted at him for cheering a goal by the wrong team.

Laurie Foster did not look happy. His ringers had been comprehensively out-rung. Chris had helped Foster's team as best he could during the first period, but Mushy's Oxford Street blues had looked the better outfit. They had the Italian kid on the wing who had set up two goals, and the copper-haired lad in goal had stopped three or four good chances.

When the over 35s took over, the Soho team were only 3–2 ahead. The blues had scored twice, both times thanks to a tall, dark, powerful striker with dreadlocks, who only played for five minutes, then left to loud applause.

The final third of the game had been the closest yet. The two dark-haired lads in midfield didn't have much class, but they did OK against the other non-League players Foster had found. Plus, they had help. Pavel's only bad moment had come when the blues had brought on a sub, a tall, elegant striker who had quickly fastened on a loose ball and smashed it home to level the scores after Foster's team had looked like they were going to run away with it.

At last, the ref decided that the pubs had been open long enough. He waved his arm, blew the whistle, and the game was over at 4–4. Foster dropped his head into his hands. Snake and Tank looked around helplessly. Moments later, the three of them left hurriedly, chased by people waving bits of paper at them.

'And that's that,' said Mr Stephens firmly. Yes, thought Chris, it just about is.

They stood up to go and join the Fiorentini clan, who were massed by the touchline, applauding Nicky's cousins as if they had just won the FA Cup. Nicky was boasting about the two goals he had set up. Russell Jones threw his goalkeeping gloves into a bag and sat back on the bench, stretching out his muscles. He gave Chris the thumbs up.

'Is that it, then?' asked Aunt Helen. 'No more trouble from any of those nasty men?'

Chris got the impression that she was asking more on Mrs Davidov's behalf than on her own. She and Pyotr were looking down towards the pitch, where Pavel was shaking hands with his team mates. Mrs Davidov still looked tense and worried, but she smiled bravely.

Chris, looking back over his shoulder, wondered what to say.

'I think I can answer that,' said a woman's voice.

Jumping slightly, Chris turned to the front again, to be faced with a young woman in jeans and a sweatshirt, with a dark blue jacket on top. She reached into a pocket and pulled out a small black wallet, which she flicked open.

'DS Janet Marsh, Metropolitan Police,' she said with a smile.

The voice was vaguely familiar, as was the face, but Chris couldn't quite place her.

'Don't you recognise me without the wig?' she asked, grinning. It still took Chris a moment.

'Sandy?'

The woman nodded. 'Foster dropped me off so I could get changed for our 'big celebration'. He knows 'Sandy' doesn't like football that much. Mind you, I don't think he's in a celebrating mood any more.'

'I think you're right . . .' said Chris.

'Anyway, he showed me where he was hiding the organiser, so that's useful. He doesn't trust Gloria these days, not after she lost it before.'

The penny dropped.

'Gloria's an undercover cop too?'

'Yes. We sneaked her into Foster's organisation a few months ago. We have evidence of all kinds of things, thanks to her, and I bet there's even more in the hidden safe at his house where he put the organiser. When this football scam came up, we thought we might pull in some other fish too. Who would have guessed we'd get Herr Koln?'

'Oh,' was the only comment Chris could muster at first. He was finishing off the jigsaw in his head. 'Is Illyana another undercover cop?'

'No,' said Marsh. 'It's me. Different wig. I was trying to persuade Pavel to help me get Foster. I put it around that I was with the Russian mob to get access. I didn't expect Koln to be here in person.'

Chris could feel the last few pieces fall into place. 'So, when Mushy grabbed the bag in Oxford Street –'

'I'd called Gloria and told her to bring it to the meet I had with Pavel at the Odessa. I thought with the computer and Pavel we'd have a case. But Pavel got spooked when Mushy nicked it, and thought it was some kind of double-cross. Very paranoid, these Russians. He didn't realise I was on his side.'

'Who did?' asked Chris.

'Anyway, I just thought I'd let you know that you were a great help. With any luck, the stuff on the organiser will help us arrest Koln, or at least get him thrown out of the country.'

As the policewoman said this, Pavel Davidov joined them, putting his big arms round his wife and son.

'Is my husband in any trouble?' asked Mrs Davidov.

'Good Lord, no!' 'Sandy' replied.

'But I could have been in great trouble with the club if not for your help,' the big defender told Chris. 'Either Foster or Koln could have made me –' He left the sentence unfinished. 'I would have been in big trouble with United just for playing here today, without permission. But it will all be all right now, I think.'

'I'm sure it will,' said Aunt Helen. 'Just get this money nonsense sorted out, Pavel.'

'I think it is in hand,' Pavel said, and he winked at Chris. 'Now, I have to go. Ruud Gullit says he will give me a lift to Stamford Bridge. The kick-off is getting a bit close.'

Chris could see the Chelsea manager at the foot of the stairs below them, looking a little anxious to be gone.

'He would never have done this if he was not such good friends with Sean Priest,' Pavel explained to no-one in particular. 'And Sean only called him because he trusts you, Chris.'

Chris blushed. He wasn't used to this much praise. And it had been a team effort, from the Fiorentinis who had driven down to bring support and a couple of useful players to balance out Foster's ringers, to the way people back in Oldcester had worked the phones to find Sean in Scotland and get him to help.

'Who was it persuaded Teddy Sheringham to turn out?' asked Mr Stephens.

'Actually he came on his own,' said Chris. 'He got fed up of seeing his face all over those tacky blue posters, so he came to see what was going on.'

'And found himself caught up in another of your dumb plans.'

Chris nodded. His father sighed and shoved his hands in his pockets, as if he couldn't decide whether to pat Chris on the back or strangle him. Chris half-hoped all the praise he had received might mean that he would escape too much punishment from his father. Or maybe not.

'One thing, though,' Pavel added as he prepared to leave. 'Sean says he is going to kill you for interrupting his holiday when he gets back.'

Nicky and Russell laughed loudly across the stairway, having been listening in. Chris knew they couldn't wait for training to start again.

'Well,' said DS Marsh, 'I'd better be going. It's nice to have a case like this that works out so neatly.'

Everyone murmured their agreement. It did seem as if things had turned out all right. Only Chris was wondering how complicated Marsh's tricky cases could be.

'Actually,' said Chris, 'I need to have a word with you about that organiser . . . the one with the stuff about Koln on it?'

'The one in Foster's safe, yes,' said DS Marsh, but her smile was fading as she saw the expression on Chris's face.

Chris took a deep breath, wondering where to start. With the fake organiser? With the real one, which Mushy had and which Koln was chasing, but which didn't have any data on it because someone had tried to download it? Or with Toby, who Chris was pretty sure had the information stashed on a computer somewhere, wondering what it was?

'Let me see if I can make this simple,' he began. 'You see, we'd just beaten Southampton six-two and we went to this restaurant . . .'

WE NEED YOUR HELP . . .

to ensure that we bring you the books you want –

– and no stamp required!

All you have to do is complete the attached questionnaire and return it to us. The information you provide will help us to keep publishing the books you want to read. The completed form will also give us a better picture of who reads the Team Mates books and will help us continue marketing these books successfully.

TEAM MATES QUESTIONNAIRE

Please ***circle*** *the answer that applies to you and add more information where necessary.*

SECTION ONE: ABOUT YOU

1.1 Are you?

Male / Female

1.2 How old are you? .... years

1.3 Which other Team Mates books have you read?

Overlap
The Keeper
Foul!
Giant Killers
Sweeper
Offside
Penalty

1.4 What do you spend most of your pocket money on? (Please give details.)

Books ______________________________

____

Magazines ______________________________

____

Toys ______________________________

____

Computer games ______________________________

____

Other ______________________________

____

1.5 Do you play football?

Yes / No

1.6 Which football team do you support, if any?

____

1.7 Who is your favourite football player, if you have one?

____

SECTION TWO: ABOUT THE BOOKS

2.1 Where do you buy your Team Mates book/s from?

W H Smith
John Menzies
Waterstones
Dillons
Books Etc
A supermarket (say which one) ______________
A newsagent (say which one) ______________
Other ______________________________

2.2 Which is your favourite Team Mates story and what do you like most about it?

____

____

____

2.3 How did you find out about Team Mates books?

Friends
Magazine
Store display
Gift
Other ____________________________

2.4 Would you like to know more about the Team Mates series of books?

Yes / No

If yes, would you like to receive more information direct from Virgin Publishing?

Yes / No

If yes, please fill in your name and address below:

____

____

____

____

2.5 What do you find exciting and interesting about the Team Mates stories?

____

____

____

SECTION THREE: ADDITIONAL INFORMATION

3.1 Are there any other comments about Team Mates you would like to make?

____

____

____

____

Thank you for completing this questionnaire. Now tear it out of the book – carefully! – put it in an envelope and send it to:

Team Mates
FREEPOST LON 3453
London
W10 5BR

No stamp is required if you are resident in the UK.